THE CALLBACK

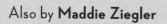

Also by **Maddie Ziegler**

The Maddie Diaries
The Audition
The Competition

MADDIE ZIEGLER

THE CALLBACK

with Julia DeVillers

ALADDIN
New York   London   Toronto   Sydney   New Delhi

ALADDIN

An imprint of Simon & Schuster Children's Publishing Division

1230 Avenue of the Americas, New York, New York 10020

First Aladdin paperback edition Octover 2019

Text and interior illustrations copyright © 2018 by M, M and M, Inc.

Cover illustration copyright © 2018 by Magdalina Dianova

Also available in an Aladdin hardcover edition.

All rights reserved, including the right of reproduction in whole or in part in any form.

ALADDIN and related logo are registered trademarks of Simon & Schuster, Inc.

For information about special discounts for bulk purchases, please contact Simon & Schuster Special Sales at 1-866-506-1949 or business@simonandschuster.com.

The Simon & Schuster Speakers Bureau can bring authors to your live event. For more information or to book an event contact the Simon & Schuster Speakers Bureau at 1-866-248-3049 or visit our website at www.simonspeakers.com.

Book designed by Laura Lyn DiSiena

The text of this book was set in Miller Text.

Manufactured in the United States of America 0919 OFF

10 9 8 7 6 5 4 3 2 1

Library of Congress Cataloging-in-Publication Data

Names: Ziegler, Maddie, author. | DeVillers, Julia, author.

Title: The callback / by Maddie Ziegler with Julia DeVillers.

Description: First Aladdin hardcover edition. | New York : Aladdin, 2018. | Series: Maddie Ziegler ; 2 | Summary: Harper McCoy, twelve, joins the school musical hoping to get past "dancer's block," but her Dance Starz teammates are not pleased, especially since they will soon compete against their biggest rivals, The Belles, in Regionals.

Identifiers: LCCN 2018012756 (print) | LCCN 2018018883 (eBook) | ISBN 9781481486415 (eBook) | ISBN 9781481486392 (hardcover)

Subjects: | CYAC: Dance—Fiction. | Competition (Psychology—Fiction. Cliques (Sociology)—Fiction. | Musicals—Fiction. | Theater—Fiction. | Family life—Florida—Fiction. | Florida—Fiction. | BISAC: JUVENILE FICTION / Performing Arts / Dance. | JUVENILE FICTION / Social Issues / Friendship. | JUVENILE FICTION / Social Issues / New Experience.

Classification: LCC PZ7.1.Z54 (eBook) | LCC PZ7.1.Z54 Cal 2018 (print) | DDC [Fic]—dc23

LC record available at https://lccn.loc.gov/2018012756

ISBN 9781481486408 (pbk)

5.6.7.8

Illustrations by Maddie Ziegler

I'm standing just offstage, waiting for my big moment. I'm with my competition dance team. I'm really nervous, because I'm about to do a trick that I've never done before. The most complicated leap that my dance team, DanceStarz, has ever attempted! I whip off my pink, white, and gold dance team jacket, which only the five dancers on the select competition team get to wear. Underneath, my costume shined with thousands of tiny sequins, just like I was going to shine onstage!

"You can do it, Harper! Love you, Harper!" My new teammates are encouraging, but I know they're thinking the same thing I am: This is nearly impossible! How can a twelve-year-old pull off this stunt?

My teammates run out on the stage and get into their positions. The music begins. Five . . . six . . . seven . . . eight . . .

I run onto the stage, my head held high. I push off my left leg powerfully, and then stretch my legs out into a split.

"Harper McCoy! Harper McCoy!" someone calls out from the audience. I smile my best smile, secretly thrilled I have fans out there who would call my name.

I leap higher than I ever have before! I leap over my teammates, who are crouched down underneath me. I leap over Riley, over Trina—and even over Megan, who looks surprised that I made it.

"Harper's leaping! She's leaping!" my teammate Riley whispers loudly.

I am! I'm now leaping over Lily, my best friend on my dance team! And then my little sister, Hailey! And my dance teacher, Vanessa! Wait a minute. And then I leap over my dog, Mo!

Wait. What?

Why are my dance teacher and my dog onstage with me? I lose my focus and land on the stage. I fall forward flat on my face. I'm facedown! Everyone is laughing at me!

"Ha!" my teammate Riley laughs really hard. "Ha-ha! Harper's sleeping!"

Wait, sleeping? Not leaping? I opened my eyes and snapped

out of it. I was facedown, all right—on my school desk. I lifted my head up to see my classmates looking at me and cracking up. Including Riley.

"Harper's sleeping!" Riley whispers even louder this time, and more people turn to look at me. Including my teacher.

Oops. I hadn't been leaping. I'd been sleeping. In my first-period English class.

"Harper McCoy. I apologize if my lesson isn't stimulating enough to keep you awake," Mrs. Elliott said. "Please see me after class."

I slumped down in my chair. I could see Riley, a few desks over, cracking up with her friend. I'd been at my new school only a few weeks, and already I was embarrassing myself. Ugh. The rest of the class period I did my best to focus. However, I did yawn a few times when my teacher was looking the other way.

After class was over, I went up to my teacher's desk.

"I'm sorry, Mrs. Elliott," I mumbled. "I didn't mean to fall asleep. I was up late last night."

"I understand," Mrs. Elliott answered and smiled at me. *Whew!* I was relieved she was being so nice about it. Then she continued, "I just wanted to check to see if everything is all right."

"Yeeessss . . ." I hesitated. Mrs. Elliott smiled again, looking so kind and understanding that everything just spilled out of me. "It's just that, well, I only moved here a month ago, so I'm still getting used to everything! Florida! It's so much hotter, and my new house? It's a nice house and my new bedroom is really cute, but it's still weird, and starting a new school with all these new people? Plus . . ."

I paused to take a breath. I knew I was babbling, and I just couldn't stop. My teacher just waited.

"I'm at a new studio—I mean, it's fun and I love it, but there's so much pressure on me at DanceStarz."

My teacher's eyebrows shot up.

"Dance?" she asked me.

"Yeah at DanceStarz Academy. I'm on the select team, called the Squad. Back in Connecticut, I'd been on the competition team, but here? It's on a whole new level. I mean, I love it, but it's intense."

I was babbling.

"Basically, I'm tired. I'm really sorry I fell asleep," I finished lamely.

"Harper. Do you, by chance, do musical theater?" Mrs. Elliott asked me.

"Musical theater? Sure." I nodded. "And jazz, tap, ballet, contemporary, and lyrical. And tumbling, although I'm not the best at it."

"Can you do pirouettes?"

"Oh, yeah," I said, confidently. I thought that was a little bit of a random question, but hey, turns were my specialty. Plus, I was really happy to have the focus shift from me getting in trouble for sleeping in class! Maybe I could distract her. "Do you want to see me pirouette?"

When she nodded, before she could say anything, I went over to the front of the classroom. I took my prep and then held my plié for a second, making sure my technique was perfect. Then I pulled up, spotting six consecutive turns with a graceful landing. *Nailed it!* I posed and looked over at Mrs. Elliott, who looked equally surprised and happy.

"Fate works in mysterious ways," Mrs. Elliott said. "I was really feeling the pressure."

Wait, she was feeling the pressure?

"I'm sure you've heard that the middle school play will be *The Little Mermaid*," she continued.

"I saw the posters for tryouts a couple weeks ago," I said. "Of course, I'd be happy to go see it."

That wasn't a punishment for falling asleep. I love *The Little Mermaid*.

"Oh, I don't want you to see it," Mrs. Elliott said, laughing. "I want you to be in it."

"In it?" I was totally confused.

"We have a dance number in the show that I believe is a highlight," Mrs. Elliott explained. "And I say this modestly, well, because I choreographed it myself."

She lowered her eyes dramatically.

"Uh," I said. "Cool?"

"However, our dancer had to drop out of the play yesterday," Mrs. Elliott said. "I need to replace her. And I think you would be perfect doing that featured dance solo she was supposed to do."

A featured dance solo. A featured dance solo!

"I want to be clear that your answer is in no way related to you dozing off in class today or English class," Mrs. Elliott said. "There's no pressure to say yes. However, you're not off the hook. I'd like to see a few extra paragraphs on the essay due next week to show effort."

I already had so much going on, but . . . *The Little Mermaid* would be so fun! It was one of my favorite movies. And getting picked for a solo without really having to audition felt really good. A solo that wasn't going to be part of a competition.

Plus, maybe it would be a chance to shine at my new school.

"Yes," I said. "I'll do it."

Mrs. Elliott's face lit up.

With Mrs. Elliott thanking me profusely, I left the room to go to lunch.

"Ack!" I bumped right into Lily. She was waiting in the hallway. She usually met me after English so we could walk into lunch together. I'd met Lily the day of my DanceStarz audition, and I was happy she'd made the Squad too. And we went to the same school—so we were newbies there, too. We didn't have any of the same classes, but at least we got to have lunch together.

"Oh, sorry you had to wait for me," I apologized. "Mrs. Elliott wanted to talk to me."

"I didn't mean to spy, but that didn't look like talking," Lily said. "That looked like dancing!"

I lowered my voice into a whisper.

"It was," I whispered. "That was so unexpected."

I told her how Mrs. Elliot had asked me to be in the school musical. And how I'd said yes.

"Harper, it sounds fun, but aren't you already crazy busy?" Lily asked.

"Yeah," I said. "I probably should have said no, but . . . it actually sounds really cool. It's just one dance. Plus, I'll be a solo dancer! And I love *The Little Mermaid*!"

"I love *The Little Mermaid* too," Lily agreed—and then I

realized something. Maybe Lily would want the chance to be in the musical, herself.

"Oh my gosh, I'm so selfish," I said. "Do you want to try to dance in the show? We can ask Mrs. Elliott."

"Uh, no, thank you," Lily said firmly. "I have enough with the Squad and helping at Sugar Plums. The store is getting so busy!"

I was happy the store was doing great. Lily moved here because her parents bought a really cute frozen yogurt store. It was right next to DanceStarz, which made it super convenient for us to go over after lessons. Lily's parents even let me test out new flavors sometimes, like this berry hibiscus one I was now obsessing over.

"I'll come watch you in the play, though," Lily said. "A dance solo! Ooh, I wonder what you're going to wear! Maybe you're a mermaid!"

"Maybe!" I said. "Or maybe I'm something awful. Like an enormous clam."

"Maybe that's why the other dancer dropped out. She was like, *I am not wearing an enormous clam*," Lily said. We both started laughing.

I was still smiling when I walked into the lunchroom. We sat with Riley, who was one of the other three girls on our dance team. Our other teammates, Megan and Trina, went to our rival school. The three of them had been dancing together since they were little, and their nickname was the Bunheads. If you think it was hard being new in that situation—you're right.

Despite all that, at our first competition, we'd come together and come in third! I think we were getting along a little better outside of the studio too, which was nice.

Riley was sitting with her friend Naima, who also went to DanceStarz and was on a different dance team. I put my lunch on the table and Lily and I sat down across from them.

"Look who's awake from her nap!" Riley laughed.

"Huh?" Lily looked back and forth at us, confused.

In the excitement of getting to do the solo dance in the play, I'd forgotten about the falling-asleep-in-class part. Ugh.

"Oh, you didn't hear?" Riley said. "Harper fell asleep in English and she was, like, drooling all over her desk."

"WHAT? I wasn't drooling," I protested as Riley and Naima were cracking up.

"And making little snoring noises," Naima said cheerfully. "Our teacher was like, 'Harper! You are embarrassing yourself! Wake yourself up!'"

"That is not what happened," I assured Lily while pouring

my granola into the yogurt a little too aggressively. Granola spluttered over the side.

"How would you know that if you were asleep?" Riley asked.

She had a point, but I did not even want to think about it.

"And then Mrs. Elliott made her stay after class!" Naima said, like it was some hot take. "Harper, did you get in trouble? Did you get detention?

"Detention?" Riley asked. "Uh-oh, do you have to miss Squad rehearsal? Should I text Megan and Trina that you're not coming?"

She pulled out her phone to text the other two Bunheads and waved it at me tauntingly.

"Ahem." One of the lunch monitors appeared behind her. "Cell phones need to stay in your locker. If I see that again, I'll have to give you detention."

Lily and I glanced at each other, but then had to look away so we wouldn't crack up.

"Sorry," Riley muttered and shoved her phone back into her pocket.

"Karma!" Lily said. "You might be the one getting detention, not Harper."

"Whatever," Riley muttered.

"Harper, if you didn't get detention, why did Elliott make you stay after? Ooh! Is she going to flunk you?" Naima said breathlessly. "If you flunk English, will your parents be like, *Oh no, Harper is grounded from all extracurriculars,* and then you'll get kicked off the Squad, and no offense, that would be great because I could try out for your spot!"

"Gee, thanks, Naima, for your support. But I'm not flunking English," I said, aggressively stirring my yogurt so hard it spilled over the edges. "And I'm not giving up my spot."

"Yeah, nobody's taking Harper's spot," Lily declared. "Harper is one of the very best dancers in the whole studio."

"I'm not flunking English," I said, slamming my yogurt down on the table. "And I'm not giving up my spot."

"Yeah, nobody's taking Harper's spot," Lily said. "Harper is one of the very best dancers in the whole studio."

"Do you think you're going to get the solo, Harper?" Naima asked me, totally putting me on the spot.

"I . . ." Before I could come up with an answer for that, Riley jumped in.

"Megan is getting the solo," Riley said. "It's totally going to be Megan."

"I think it's going to be Harper," Lily said. "Have you seen her newest turn series? It's epic."

"All five of us are good competitors," I said diplomatically. "We all might have a shot."

"Uh, not Riley!" Naima said, a little too cheerfully.

Riley looked sadly at her hand. I did feel sorry for her. Her hand was definitely healing, but still not 100 percent.

At our first competition, things had gotten a little stressful. The Bunheads' former best friends, nicknamed "The Bells," had joined a rival team, Energii. Right before DanceStarz was about to go on, there was drama and Megan had accidentally stepped on Riley's hand. We had to change up our whole routine at the last second. Riley had healed enough for her to dance, but only as long she didn't put pressure on her hand, which meant she still couldn't do any of her show-stopping tricks she was known for, like her hand-walking and handsprings. Not to mention her jazz hands.

"Riley is still a good dancer," I pointed out. "So are Lily and Trina."

"Oh, you know it's pretty much going to be between you and Megan," Naima said. "Everyone on our team is talking about it. Most people are betting on Megan."

Vanessa was going to assign each of us a solo dance we would work on ourselves. After we learned it, she would have us "audition" for the solo part in the next competition.

"I'm going to try my best," I said, and took a sip of my lemonade juice pack to calm down the butterflies in my stomach. "I'm sure we all will."

Any solo you get to perform at a competition is a big deal. But this one felt even more special. Since the Squad was the first ever select team at DanceStarz, this would be the FIRST EVER solo in the entire history of the Squad. The person who got this solo would basically be making DanceStarz history!

And I wanted it.

I wanted the solo really badly.

Lily kicked me under the table, and then tilted her head toward the clock over the lunch table. 11:10! We had a tradition, ever since the first time we met. We both watched the clock until it turned. . . .

11:11—make a wish! I saw Lily close her eyes. I closed my eyes too and made a wish.

I wished I would get the competition solo.

I wondered if Lily was wishing for that, too.

After school, I jumped in the front passenger seat of my mom's SUV. I had two classes at DanceStarz today: Squad rehearsal and Advanced Jazz.

"How was your day?" Mom asked me.

"Good," I said, buckling my seat belt. "Kind of weird."

"Harper!" My sister popped up from the backseat.

Speaking of "kind of weird." Hailey had a bunch of different kinds of braids on her head. One was crooked, one was falling apart, one was poking out of the top of her head like a unicorn horn—and don't even get me started on all the wispies sprouting from them.

"Lean your head back on the seat," Hailey said. "I can do your hair for you for dance."

"Um. Thanks, but no?" I tried.

"But I've been practicing!" Hailey said, shaking her head. "Look at all the different braids I can do! Regular, French, fishtail!"

"I see that," I said diplomatically. "Lots of . . . unusual braids. Uh, my hair is a little different from yours."

Our hair wasn't actually that different—we both had brown hair, although hers was thicker than mine and she wore it wavy, while I usually wore mine straighter. I tried to think of another excuse.

"Pleeeease, Harper, I watched so many videos on braiding," she begged. "I need to practice on somebody who isn't me. I can't make them look good on myself."

Well, at least she recognized that. My mom also gave me a look that said *You really should say yes and be nice to your sister.*

"Fine," I said. I wanted to put my mom in a good mood for what I was about to ask her. Plus, I was really fast at putting my hair up in a bun—and when I had to redo the braids, I had everything with me in my dance bag I needed. Hailey leaned over to brush my hair. It was actually kind of relaxing, and I closed my eyes to chill.

"So, Harper, why did you say your day was weird?"

My mom's question snapped me back to reality.

"Oh!" I turned to look at my mom, which was a mistake because Hailey yanked my hair. "Ouch!"

"Don't move!" Hailey ordered. "Your braid will get crooked. I'm trying to get it perfectly straight."

"My English teacher asked me to be part of the school musical," I told my mom as I tilted my head back.

"The school musical? Don't you have a lot on your plate already?" Mom asked.

"It's only one dance I have to do—but it's a solo," I said. "I don't even have to audition! I danced a little bit for her"—I conveniently left out the part about me being there since I fell asleep in class—"and then she asked if I would do it. They're doing *The Little Mermaid*—ouch!"

"Sorry!" Hailey said, yanking at my hair. "French braids are tricky. I love *The Little Mermaid*. Are you Ariel? I'll start learning mermaid-style braids for your hair!"

"Whoa, Hailey, just a minute," my mom said. "Harper, a musical? Won't this interfere with dance and school?"

"Miss Elliott said I could rehearse when I don't have

dance," I said. "And during lunch or study hall if I want."

"Woo! My sister's the star of the school play!" Hailey said. "Can I have your autograph, please?"

"I'm not the star." I laughed, leaning back on the headrest so Hailey could reach the top of my head and tie off the braid. "I'm not playing Ariel."

"Who are you going to be?" Hailey asked.

"I don't know," I said. "All I know is . . . I'm dancing. I might just be a random fish."

"HarperFish!" Hailey started laughing. I could see her in my side mirror making fish faces at me.

"Hailey, enough. Harper, I don't know that it's a great idea to take anything else on right now," Mom started. She paused a minute and pulled the car up in front of the dance studio. "But . . ."

I grabbed my dance duffel and waited for the verdict.

"Your father and I do want you to be more involved in your school. Since it was your teacher who asked . . ." She sighed. "If you think you can handle it, I'll give my permission."

"Awesome!" I said, jumping out of the car. "Thanks, Mom!"

"We're going to the grocery store," Mom called out the window. "We'll be back before you're finished!"

I waved good-bye and ran into the studio, before Mom

could change her mind about the school play. Harper had her face pressed up to the window, making fish faces at me, and I was in such a good mood I squished my lips into a fish face right back at her.

Yay! I would be in *The Little Mermaid*, dancing a solo, and I didn't even have to audition! Double yay! I was smiling as I pushed the door open to the studio.

However, as soon as I entered the studio, all of my thoughts of a school musical solo were replaced by thoughts of a DANCESTARZ SOLO. That was the one I really wanted.

"Hi, Harper!" the assistant who was working the front desk called out to me. The DanceStarz logo blinked over the top of the reception desk as if it were also saying hello to me.

"Hi!" I said back. I needed to get my focus back on the most important solo I could be dancing: the competition solo.

The studio was already busy, with dancers stretching on the floor, a few little toddlers bopping around the kiddie play area, and moms chatting away. DanceStarz Academy was really cool. I was still getting used to the differences from my studio back in Connecticut where I'd been going to since I was three. Like a lot of things in Florida, DanceStarz was a lot brighter than my old studio with huge floor-to-ceiling windows overlooking palm trees that let the blazing sun shine through.

"Hi, Harper!" some of the Tiny Team girls called out to me. The Tiny Team was our youngest team for girls under six. They were so cute! Being on the Squad felt a teeny bit like being famous. Not famous-famous, obviously, but famous in the dance studio. I knew a lot of the younger girls looked up to us. I stopped and said hi to them and admired one little girl's new tutu.

"I like your hair," one of the little girls said.

"Oh, thanks!" I said. I'd forgotten Hailey had done my braid. She must have done a good job.

"I have to go to rehearsal now!" I told them. "Make sure you practice too."

I went into the changing room. A couple people were in it, getting ready. I had already slid on my leotard underneath in the car: a violet-colored cami one. I pulled my olive T-shirt dress over my head and kicked off my sneakers. I stuffed the dress and sneakers in one of the compartments of my dance duffel bag. I went down the hallway to Studio B, where we had Squad rehearsals. The Bunheads were waiting outside the closed door for the class in it to be let out.

At first, they didn't see me. Megan was whispering something to Trina and Riley. Megan was kind of the leader of the Bunheads. She had her curly brown hair back in a low ponytail, and was wearing a black lace back crop top with dance shorts. Riley had her strawberry blond hair in two pigtails and was wearing a red draped tank top and black cropped leggings. Trina had her black hair up in a bun and was wearing a classic pale pink leotard.

"Hi!" I said to the girls.

Megan, Riley, and Trina turned to me and all started giggling. At me.

"What's so funny?" I challenged them.

When I'd started at the studio, I'd been really intimidated by Megan, Riley, and Trina. Now that I'd gotten to know them better, I was . . . well, I was still a little intimidated by Megan, actually. But I was much better at standing up for myself. Like now. Maybe Riley had told them about my falling asleep in class today and that's why they were laughing. Well, I was going to refuse to let them embarrass me about that.

"You do you, Harper." Megan was still cracking up.

The door opened, and while the previous class was filing out, I went inside the studio. As I entered the three-sided mirrored room I realized what they were laughing about. They weren't laughing about my falling asleep in class. They were laughing at my hair.

The braid was literally sticking straight on the top of my

head like an antenna. Agh! I'd walked through the whole studio like this! I felt my face turn pink. I turned my head from side to side.

Okay, maybe it was a little funny.

"All right, now I see," I rushed to explain to the other girls, who were putting their stuff in their cubbies. "Hailey did my hair! Hailey is practicing braiding."

"I'm thinking she needs more practice." Riley snorted.

"True," I said. "It's a little funny."

"Harper is so sweet!" Trina said. "You let your sister do your hair, and you're so proud of her that you even wore it so you didn't hurt her feelings."

"Yeah!" I said. Well, that wasn't exactly what happened, but it was a good spin on it. "Yeah, that's what I was doing."

"You're a good big sister," Trina said.

"Thanks," I said.

"You still look ridiculous," Megan pointed out.

"I think it's cute," I lied. "Maybe I'll ask Vanessa if we can wear our hair like this for the competition!"

Everyone immediately yelled, "NO!" Even Trina couldn't be that nice.

"I'm kidding," I said, and laughed. "It does look ridiculous."

I swung my head around in circles, and the braid was so

still it didn't even move. Trina and Riley laughed out loud, and even Megan cracked a smile. I smiled a little too. I was proud of myself for not backing down from embarrassment.

I did wish I hadn't walked through the lobby like this, but . . . Anyway, I needed to get my hair dance-ready ASAP, before Vanessa arrived!

"I'd better make my hair look normal," I said, and ran over to my dance bag. I reached up and pulled the elastics out of my hair. Hailey had put them in so tightly it was a challenge to free my hair, and one of the bands broke. I opened up my dance bag again.

I sorted through my dance necessities:

Hairspray

Extra leo

Bobby pins

Tights

Hairbrush

Bandages

Tape for my feet

Toe pads for my pointe shoes

Water bottle

A chewy cranberry granola bar

Towel
Deodorant
Stretch band

I found my hair elastics! I quickly swept my hair up into a high ponytail and started wrapping it into a topknot. Lily came in through the door, breathless. She whipped off her tank top and wiggled out of her shorts, so she was in a teal mock-turtleneck leotard. Her long black hair was up in a bun like Trina's.

"Whew!" she said. "I thought I'd be late. What'd I miss?"

"Nothing. Everyone's just stretching," I said. "And making fun of my hair. Don't ask."

"Okay." She slid her bag into the cubby. "I think your top-knot looks nice."

"Long story. Hey, guess what?" I lowered my voice. "My mom said I could be in the play. Now I just have to get the nerve up to tell Vanessa. I hope she doesn't think I'm not dedicated to the Squad."

What if Vanessa got mad that I was taking on another dance? What if she thought I wasn't going to be serious about doing a solo in the competition? How should I ask her? Lily and I sat down on the floor and did leg stretches in silence as I thought about these things.

When Vanessa walked in the room, I jumped up.

"Vanessa—"

"Vanessa!" Megan jumped up faster and ran up to our teacher. I sighed and stood back to give her some privacy, while I waited my turn. Megan spoke animatedly, and Vanessa nodded and Megan grinned. When they were finished, Vanessa turned to me.

"Harper?" she asked. Megan went back to the Bunheads on the other side of the room.

"Vanessa, I have a question about . . . um . . ." I hesitated nervously. "A solo—"

"Yes! The answer is yes," Vanessa said.

Oh! Huh? Did I even ask my question? Did she read my mind?

"Megan just asked the same question," Vanessa said.

Huh? Megan asked about being in her school play?

"Let me make an announcement to everyone." She clapped her hands. "Squad!"

I was completely confused now. Everyone came over and stood in front of her in a semicircle. Lily stood next to me and squeezed my hand.

"Yes, today is the day," Vanessa announced. "I'm going to

tell you what dances you each will be given for your solos today!"

Oh! That solo. She thought I was asking about the competition solo. Well, that wasn't the question I was asking, but I suddenly felt really excited. It definitely was a question I wanted answered! All thoughts of my school musical disappeared as I jumped around with everyone else, excited.

"Each of you will be assigned a solo dance, tailored to what I see as your strengths . . ."

Everyone smiled.

". . . and also including a few skills I think you should work to improve."

We all looked at each other like, *yikes.*

"After we have worked on your dances, each of you will perform for me and we'll determine which one of you will perform your solo at regionals."

Everyone looked away from one another. We did love being a team now, but we still had the same goal—and we all knew only one of us could get that spot.

"First up, Lily!" Vanessa said.

Lily stepped forward and gave a nervous grin.

"Your solo dance will be an acro routine called 'Flip it.'"

I looked to Lily to see her reaction, but her face didn't show anything. I thought she'd be happy with that. She'd grown up taking only ballet, but had told us she liked tumbling and gymnastics more now. So acro—short for acrobatics—should be fun for her.

"Thank you," Lily said, and stepped back in line.

Vanessa said. "Riley, your solo dance will be a jazz piece, called 'Pizzazz.'"

Riley seemed pretty happy with that. She had really good facials and performance skills. Besides hip-hop, jazz would be a good fit for her high-energy dancing. "Trina! Your solo will be a tap dance, titled 'In Sync.'"

"Yay!" She clapped her hands. Everyone laughed a little. A tap dancing solo was totally up Trina's alley. Her footwork was amazing, and her timing was really good.

Then Vanessa looked at me. I was practically dying of suspense.

"Harper, your dance will be a lyrical piece titled 'Taking the Leap,'" Vanessa said.

Awesome. Lyrical was pretty much my favorite style of dance. It was fluid and flowy from step to step, which was easier for me than focusing on precise, fast movements. Hopefully, with a name like "Taking the Leap," that meant I'd be able to show off my leaps and turns.

"Thank you!" I said, smiling.

"Megan," Vanessa continued. "You'll do a contemporary routine called 'Me Over You.'"

"Yesss," Megan said, and pumped her fist. She obviously liked that one. Our group routine also was contemporary, but the category had a really wide range. Contemporary did have good focus on technique, and Megan was really technically on point and had some super-impressive tricks.

She was going to be hard to beat.

"I'll be working with each of you privately to learn your routines," Vanessa explained. "It's going to be a lot of hard work, but also a lot of fun."

There were nods all around the room. We were here for the hard work. We were ready!

"Meanwhile, we'll continue working on our group routine," Vanessa said. "Along with a solo, we'll be competing at regionals as a group with our top-three routine, 'Awaken'!"

We all cheered.

"However, I want to see us place even higher," Vanessa said, and we all nodded. "So today we'll work on some basic skills to elevate the routine."

She had us all go to the barres lining the mirror. I went to stand beside Lily. The Bunheads stood together at the other end.

"What do you think?" I asked Lily.

"You must be excited about getting lyrical," Lily said, and I nodded.

"And you must be excited you got acro," I told her. "You've been wanting to do more tumbling."

"Yeah," she said. "That's the good part. It could be fun."

She didn't look as happy as I thought she would. I frowned. I'd have to talk to her more about that, later. We all put our hands on the barre and went through the ballet positions.

I caught a glimpse of Lily's face in the mirror. She looked unhappy, but I also knew she wasn't a big fan of ballet, so maybe she was just focusing really hard. You have to be precise with every single movement. I found it intense, but because I had to focus on my body movements it was a nice break from everyday stress.

"And pliés!" Vanessa commanded. "Plié combos!"

We went into ronde de jambes, then bent them into fondus.

"Feet look good, Harper!" Vanessa came down the line.

I smiled. I'd been having a hard time keeping up with the quick footwork that DanceStarz had been becoming known for. Fortunately, I was born with good feet for dancing—high arches so I could hyperextend them—so when the moves were slower, my feet at least did what I wanted them to do. Today's class was turning out great. I was happy that I'd have a lyrical solo. And most important, I'd gotten a compliment from Vanessa!

When class ended, we were all achy in a good way from working hard, and I was in a really good mood.

"I posted a sheet to sign-up for your solo rehearsals," Vanessa announced. "Everyone please sign up for three."

Everyone ran over to the wall with the sign-up sheet. Vanessa walked over to the other side of the room. This would be a good time to talk to Vanessa about my commitment to the school musical. Instead of standing in line, I started to go over to Vanessa.

Megan spotted me and came running up beside me.

"What's up?" she asked. "Are you excited about getting lyrical?"

"Definitely," I told her. "Excuse me, I need to go to ask Vanessa something."

"Oh, me too," Megan said. She then picked up her pace and virtually knocked me out of the way to get to Vanessa first.

"Yes?" Vanessa looked at both of us.

"Vanessa," Megan jumped right in. "I'm really excited I get to do a contemporary dance solo opportunity. I want to get started right away, so if you think there's anything in particular I should be working on, please let me know."

"I'll let you know in your private lesson," Vanessa said firmly. "But I appreciate your enthusiasm."

"Oh, yeah!" Megan nodded vigorously. "I'm devoting every spare minute I have besides homework to rehearsing for this solo! Every. Minute."

Oh, great.

"And I also appreciate your dedication," Vanessa said. Then she turned to me. "Harper? Do you need something?"

Megan hovered, listening nearby. I gave her a look that she ignored. There was no way I could tell Vanessa about my part in the show right now, with Megan eavesdropping and just after Megan's whole *one hundred percent devoted* speech. I wracked my brain trying to think of something to say.

"Uh . . . nope. I mean, nope, thank you."

Smooth, Harper, I thought to myself as I backed away. Urgh. Vanessa gave me a strange look. I ran to the cubbies and basically buried my face in my duffel bag, pretending to look for something until I was sure both Vanessa and the Bunheads had left the room.

Then I went out into the lobby and looked around for Lily. I didn't see her. I waved at a few dancers I knew and went to find my mom. I spotted Hailey first, sitting on the floor with Riley's younger sister, looking at her tablet.

Hailey looked up.

"Oh, you took your braid out," Hailey said. "I was going to show Quinn. I was telling her how good I was getting. Hey, Quinn, want me to do your hair?"

"You know what, I think we have to go!" I interrupted. Quinn was Riley's sister, and she had a similar personality. I didn't think she'd be kind about Hailey's braiding skills. Or lack of skills. "Too bad."

"You're right! We do have to go." Hailey turned to Quinn. "See ya."

We both went over to the moms.

"Ready!" I said.

"Hello, Harper," Megan's mother said. "Megan said you've been finally coming along nicely with your footwork."

"Oh," I said. "Thanks?"

"Megan's inside having private lessons now," Megan's mother said. "You can't have enough training! She's so passionate about it."

"Yeah." I nodded. That was true.

"It's so exciting that you all will be performing at regionals," Riley's mother said. "Do you remember our dance regionals, Beth? Our costumes were yellow and black."

"Oh, I hated those. We looked like chickens," Megan's mother groaned.

Hailey let out a snort.

"Oh, I thought they were darling." Riley's mother clasped her hands happily. "With the little feather caps? Oh, to be young again! And being on prom court and dating the quarterback!"

"Until he dumped you for Eleanor right before nationals." Megan's mom shook her head. "You cried so much you looked like Rudolph the Red-Nosed Chicken. And then only you came in fifth with your solo. . . ."

Riley's mom scowled.

"Would you look at the time!" My mother jumped up. "Sorry! We have to run. See you next time!"

My mother basically pushed us out the door.

"Whew," she muttered under her breath. "Those two are competitive."

So are their daughters.

*H*ow was dance, Harper?" my mother asked, when we were in the car. I sat in the front seat, and Hailey sat in the back.

"Good!" I said. "Guess what? We got our solos today and I'm doing lyrical!"

"Excellent," Mom said as Hailey started clapping. "You're strong in lyrical!"

"It's called 'Taking the Leap,'" I said. "That's all I know about it, though I had to sign up for a private and she'll tell me more."

As the car pulled out of the parking space, I remembered something.

"Wait! Can I run in?" I said. "Lily ran out of dance before I got to talk to her. I need to ask her something." I really wanted to make sure Lily wasn't mad or anything. I'd had a weird feeling from her reaction to the solos announcement.

"Ughhh, I want to go home. I have things to do," Hailey said. "Can't you just text her?"

"I really need to see her," I begged my mom.

"Wait, will you help me when I get home?" Hailey asked.

"Does it involve braids?" I said, rubbing a sore spot.

"No," Hailey said. "With something else."

"You may run in quickly if you'll make it up to your sister later," Mom said.

"Okay!" I jumped out of the car and went into Sugar Plums before she could change her mind.

"Hi, Harper!" Lily's mom greeted me from behind the counter. "It's pumpkin spice season! New flavor today!"

"Thanks," I said. "But I actually was hoping to talk to Lily for one second before I went home. My mom's waiting in the car."

"She's in the break room." She smiled at me and waved toward a door near the end of the counter. "Go on back."

I went behind the counter and through the door. I'd never actually been back there, and I walked into a hallway that was filled with shelves—with huge jars of toppings like gummies, chocolate chips, and mini marshmallows. There were cans of chocolate and butterscotch syrup, cans of nuts, and an enormous tub of sprinkles. I looked at all of it, wide-eyed, for a second. Yum.

Focus, Harper, I told myself. I kept going (candy bars! cookies!) until I reached the door to the break room. When I went in, Lily was typing something on a laptop.

"Hi!" I said.

"Oh my gosh!" Lily jumped, startled. "You totally scared me."

"Sorry, your mom said I could come find you." I waved my hands toward the hallway. "Also, this is like Lily and the Chocolate Factory back here!"

Lily laughed. I was glad to see she was smiling. Looked like everything was okay, after all.

"Well, I was just saying a quick hi!" I said. "I just wanted to check with you that everything is fine! With dance and the solos and everything."

"Um." Lily's smiled dropped.

"Aren't you excited about getting an acro routine?" I babbled on. "I mean, you're so amazing at ballet, but you said you were tired of it and wanted to do more tumbling. So acro sounds perfect for you! Fun and bouncy!"

"Sure! It should be fun to rehearse!" Lily said. "Fun! Lots of fun! And lyrical is perfect for you, so everything is great! Just great!"

I could tell she was putting on a happy face.

"Lily, what's really the matter?" I asked. Lily opened her mouth to tell me something.

"A little help, here!" The back door burst open, and Lily's mom suddenly entered, carrying some boxes.

Lily and I ran over to help her.

"Just got new spoons," Lily's mother said. "Harper, would you like to test them out?"

"That's not really tempting, Mother." Lily laughed.

"No, I totally would, but I can't stay." I frowned. "My mom and Hailey are waiting in the car. Lily, I'll text you."

We hugged good-bye. I felt better about things, but I still wasn't entirely sure as I headed out into the lobby to find Lily's dad holding out a cup with a straw to me.

"This is for your mother and sister," she said. "I see them out there waiting for you. A pumpkin spice smoothie and a small bag of sour gummies."

I thanked her and headed out to the car, where my mom happily took the smoothie.

"Yay!" Hailey said when I handed her the gummies.

"Put those away for later," my mother said. "I don't want you eating too much sugar, if you're still planning on—"

"SHH!" Hailey yelled. "That's a surprise for Harper. She has to be totally surprised for it to work, Mom!"

"Okay," my mom said. "Settle down, please."

My sister was taking something very seriously. I was glad she wasn't going to braid my hair, but now I was a little concerned about what she might be involving me in.

"Everything good with Lily?" Mom asked.

"I think so," I said, glancing in the rearview mirror. I didn't want to say more, because my sister was not always good at minding her own business. "We're not in a fight or anything. Just dance stress."

"Dance stress?" Mom echoed.

"I'm good. I had a really good day at the studio," I reassured her.

"Well, your day is about to get better!" Hailey piped up from the back. "Wait till you see what we're going to do!"

When we got home, Hailey told me to put on clothes that could get messy and meet her in the kitchen for the big reveal.

I went upstairs to my bedroom to change.

My malti-poo, Mo, was sleeping on my purple circle chair and woke up when I went in.

"MO!" I said, and picked him up. He yawned, and it was the cutest thing, so I told him. "You're the cutest thing!"

I sat down on the chair and put him on my lap. I was happy Mo liked my bedroom for his hangout. I liked my new room, too. The walls and bedding were white, but I had purple touches like fluffy pillows and this chair.

I had trophies, medals, and plaques on my shelves and ribbons and award certificates on my bulletin board. You could tell by looking around my room dance was pretty much my life. I had my headbands, ribbons, and bows hanging on my closet door, and inside, old dance costumes and headgear were neatly organized.

I leaned back and sighed, and Mo leaned into me and sighed. I scratched Mo under the collar, the way he liked it. Ahh, relaxation. I needed a little break. Ahhhh . . .

"Harper!"

Ergh. So much for relaxation. Hailey was yelling up to me. I placed Mo on the floor gently and stood up.

"We are needed," I told him.

Mo looked at me, then jumped back on my purple circle chair, closed his eyes, and promptly fell asleep.

"Jealous," I told him. I sighed and went back out to the kitchen.

"Ta-da!" Hailey waved her hands at the kitchen counter,

where a bunch of pans and ingredients were set up. She was wearing one of my mom's aprons around her neck, sunglasses, and long lacy white gloves that I recognized.

"Ta-da . . . you stole my gloves?" I asked.

"Oh. Heh-heh. Remember when you said I could wear anything from your dance closet?"

"That was months ago! When we were doing Dance Challenge." I frowned.

"Oopsie." Hailey peeled the gloves off and threw them at me. I caught one, and the other flew past me. "They'll just get in the way, anyway. No, ta-da! Welcome to my new show!"

"New show?"

"Yes, the very first episode on The Hailey Channel!" she said. Hailey held up my dad's video camera to her eye and posed. "Daddy gave me his old camera. Don't I look professional? We're about to film it right here this very second. I mean, Mom won't let me put it online, but I'm going to store up all of my episodes for when I can. I'm preparing for stardom. And you're my assistant."

"I'm your assistant?" I asked.

"Obviously," she said. "Who else do I have? Mom? She'll be like, *don't do that—it could make a mess or start a fire or something.* So it's you."

"Hailey, I don't have a lot of time right now," I said.

"Fine," Hailey said, setting the video camera up on a mini tripod. "I'll make you a producer for the show. Oh, also editor, because you know how to do that."

That wasn't any more appealing.

"Harper," she whined. "I need to do my channel. I don't have dance competitions like you do. I need attention too, you know."

I tried to hold back a smile. I wasn't sure filming in our kitchen was going to mean fame and attention, but hey. She gave me her best puppy-dog eyes, and I cracked.

"I'll tape it." I sighed. "But you'll have to edit it yourself."

"Deal!" Hailey said. She ran behind the kitchen island and yelled, "Quiet on the set! Episode one, take one! Three . . . two . . . one, action! Roll 'em!"

I turned on the camera and aimed it to videotape her. Hailey turned toward the camera and flashed a huge grin.

"Welcome to *Hailey on the Daily*!" she said. "I'm Hailey and I'll be here on the daily to . . . do daily stuff! This is my sister, Harper!"

I shook my head no as Hailey waved to me to come over.

"I need you," Hailey hissed, then she plastered a smile on again. "Edit that out. Okay, we'll keep doing takes until you come over to me."

I remembered that this was not going to actually be posted

anywhere and my phone would be the only audience.

"Episode one, take two! Action! Welcome to *Hailey on the Daily*!" she said. "I'm Hailey and I'll be here on the daily to . . . do daily stuff! This is my sister, Harper!"

I went over and stood next to her.

"Look happy to be here," Hailey whisper-yelled at me.

I smiled at the camera.

"Smile like you mean it," Hailey hissed. "You look like you're in pain."

"I am smiling," I said, through gritted teeth.

"Even though she doesn't look it, Harper really is happy to be on my show," Hailey continued. "Today, I'm going to teach you how to bake and decorate a special cake! In honor of . . . my sister!"

She held up a box of cake mix and waved it at the camera.

"I'm making a mermaid cake!" Hailey said. "I picked mermaid because my sister is going to be in *The Little Mermaid*!"

"Aw." I was actually touched.

"Also, because I saw it online and it's so pretty," she added.

Hailey pulled out some ingredients she apparently had ready under the counter: eggs, butter, sugar, and some food coloring. As she cranked through the steps, the mix flew and milk splattered all over the place.

"First you mix the stuff: two cups of this, a stick of butter," Hailey said to the camera. "And now we make it mermaidy. Assistant, hand me the mermaid color: blue."

"Uh." I looked down at the very lumpy mix in the bowl. "You might want to mix it more."

"No time," Hailey whispered back. "The audience will get bored."

"I can speed it up in edits," I said, forgetting I didn't want to do edits at all.

"You said you won't edit," Hailey reminded me. "Okay! Now we mix in the mermaid blue."

She poured a drop of the blue food coloring in and frowned. Then she poured a few more.

"It's too dark. It needs to be turquoise," she said, mixing it. She read the back of the box. "Oh, it needs yellow, too."

She squeezed some yellow into the mix.

"Now it's too green," she said. She went back for the blue. Then the yellow. It started to look like a weird soup.

"Um, how much are you supposed to put in?" I asked.

"It needs to be turquoise," she declared "Mermaid color is turquoise!"

The color she had was pretty much the opposite of turquoise.

"I think it's good. Ariel's tail is greener," I said.

Hailey was stubbornly adding more and more food coloring. It was looking very liquidy, but finally she was satisfied with the color.

"There!" she said. "And now we bake it!"

She plopped everything in a pan and put it in the oven. Then we stood there.

"This could take a while," I said. "We should stop and do something else."

"Okay," Hailey said. "Let's clean up!"

I looked around at the messy bowls and utensils. Fortunately, Mo barked.

"You clean up," I said. "I need to take Mo for a walk."

I hooked up Mo to his collar and took him outside. The air was heavy and sticky, and not sunny but the kind of weather that meant it was going to rain soon. I was starting to get to know the Florida weather patterns, like that it was probably going to rain for a little bit, but then the sun could come out again. I took Mo around our block and waved hi to one of our neighbors. Yeah, Florida was starting to feel a little bit like home.

I had barely made it to our driveway before I heard Hailey calling me.

"Harper!" Hailey called out the back door. "Harper, the cake's ready!"

Wow, that went fast. I went back to the kitchen with Mo.

"Hello! *Hailey on the Daily* with your new favorite cake— Hailey's mermaid cake!" Hailey said cheerfully.

"Can you help me take it out of the oven?" Hailey asked. I pulled out some pot holders and opened the oven door. I carefully took out the round cake pan and put it on the stove. Hmm. It looked lumpy and kind of brown. I poked at it. It wasn't even solid inside—it was drippy and lumpy at the same time. Yeeks.

"It looks terrible!" Hailey said. It's not even a mermaid color!"

"Let's bake it more—" I tried to tell her, but it was too late. Hailey already had a packet of blue icing out and was pouring it on the cake.

"Hailey, no! Not until it's cooled off!" I warned.

Of course, the cake was way too hot and the icing got all gross and slid/melted all over the cake. Hailey's face fell.

"It's a disaster!" Hailey wailed. She looked really upset. "My mermaid cake is disgusting!"

"It's only your first try." I tried to console her.

"This is the first episode in my series. I used my allowance on this! It needed to be great!"

And that's when Hailey punched the cake. She was so mad she just pushed her whole hand in. Icing and goo flew up around her and all over the table and floor.

"Hailey! Stop! Mom is going to flip out!" I yelled. But then I saw the icing and goo on her face. She had huge clump of blue cake dangling from her nose. I couldn't help it, I cracked up.

"What are you laughing at?" Hailey said, still mad.

I picked up my phone and swiveled it around so she could see herself on-screen.

"Oh," she said, cracking a tiny smile. She wiped her nose off.

"Today on *Hailey on the Daily*, Hailey gets into a fight with a cake," I said in a goofy narrator voice. "But the cake fought back. Hailey has lost to a cake."

I moved the camera to the squashed cake.

"Excuse me!" Hailey said. "I didn't lose. The fight has just started."

Then she plunged her fist into the cake again. And again. It splattered up on her, and I laughed.

"See? I'm beating the cake!" Hailey said, laughing.

"It's still winning." I grinned at her. She now had brown cake and blue icing and cake goo all her face and clothes. Hailey gave me a fake glare. And then she stuck her face right into the cake.

"Dead." I laughed as Hailey smushed her face around into the cake. Then she lifted her face up and was completely covered in cake. She looked hilarious.

"Nice look," I said. Before I could stop her, Hailey ran over and gave me a huge, cakey hug.

"Ack!" I said. I wasn't expecting that—Hailey actually didn't even like hugs. Well, maybe she only liked them when she could squash goo all over me. She was giggling as she hugged me harder. "Mermaid goo!"

"I can't believe you did that to me!" I said as she hugged me.

"I'm just getting you ready for your school play," Hailey said sweetly. Then she unattached and picked up a bottle of pink-and-silver glitter sprinkles.

"Whoa!"

"JK! The top is on!!" Hailey said, pretending to sprinkle them on my head. "Tricked you . . ."

All of a sudden I felt a tickling of sprinkles on my hair.

"Uh-oh," Hailey said. "The top came off!"

"HAILEY!" I put my hand up to my head—and came up with a handful of glittery, sticky goo.

"Oops." Hailey giggled. "Hey, you're sparkling."

I shook my hair and glittery sprinkles flew out.

"What on earth is going on here?" My mom walked in the door. Hailey and I froze.

"Uh . . . ," we both said.

"Hailey got in a fight with . . ." I pointed. "The cake."

"You should see the other guy!" Hailey added, a chunk of cake falling off her ear. She tilted the cake pan toward my mom.

"Well." Mom shook her head and paused. "You definitely . . . beat up that cake. Just clean up the mess. And that includes yourselves."

"arper," Lily said to me the next day as we left English class. "Are you sparkling?"

I groaned. I'd showered twice last night to try and get all the cake goo out of my hair.

"Hailey and I made a cake with glitter sprinkles," I said. "They kind of spilled."

"On your head?" We both laughed. Yikes. "Hey, did you bring some cake for lunch? Any to share?" Lily asked, as we walked down the hall.

"Trust me, you don't want any of that cake," I said, then remembered. "And also, shoot! I'm sorry but can't go to lunch today. I have to go to something for the school musical."

"Noooo," Lily said. "You're leaving me alone with Riley and Naima. They barely talk to me."

"Sorry," I said. "Actually, I'm kind of regretting doing this. You'll be fine!"

Lily looked at me and smiled. "And you'll be great at the musical. Don't be nervous!"

"You'll be great," she said. "Don't be nervous."

I didn't know I looked it, but Lily was right, I thought as I walked up the stairs. I was nervous. Adding one more new thing to my schedule suddenly seemed overwhelming. Now I had to walk into drama club, where I didn't know anyone. The new girl once again.

I stood at the door of the auditorium for a second. I didn't think I knew anyone in here. I took a deep breath and walked in.

A group of people were all sitting onstage, mostly dangling their legs off the stage. Everyone went silent and looked at me. I remembered that moment where I'd first walked into our first DanceStarz Squad meeting and the Bunheads had looked at me and said nothing. I hated that feeling.

"Our dancer's here!" a girl called out.

"Dancer's here!" a bunch of people called out.

One girl hopped off the stage and came up the aisle toward me, carrying a juice box.

"Harper, right? Hey, I'm Ursula," she said. "Well, I'm not really Ursula, I'm Zora, but in the show I am, you know? We're staying in character today. Method acting. If I look mean, that's why. I'm really not in real life. I know Ursula is a villain, but I'm trying to find her motivation. I mean, she was banished. So maybe she has a right to be upset, you know? Wouldn't you be mad if you were banished?"

"Um." I nodded as she finally took a breath to sip the juice box. "Probably? Sure?"

"Stop hogging the dancer!" someone yelled. "Bring her over."

"ALL RIGHT, WE'RE COMING!" Zora's voice loudly boomed across the room. I could see why she had gotten the role of Ursula, the dramatic and loud sea witch. Zora waved me to follow her toward the stage, and people started introducing themselves.

"Hi, I'm Scuttle!" "I'm Aquata!" "I'm Flotsam!" "I'm King Triton!" "Hey, I'm Flounder!" Names were being thrown at me left and right. A bunch of people called out: "I'm chorus!"

"Does Mrs. Elliott know the dancer is here?" Sebastian asked.

"Yeah, she said to introduce her around. She's working with Ariel and Eric on their duet," Flounder told her.

"They're the stars, so we're eating lunch until it's our turn to rehearse."

"Yeah, that happens to us in dance with the solos and the duets." I nodded. I sat down between Flounder and Zora and opened my lunch. I just ate my turkey sandwich in silence, and listened to everyone talking around me about the play. Fortunately, I knew all of the characters, so it actually was easy to follow along. King Triton, Ariel's powerful father. Scuttle, the cheerful seagull. Flounder, the awkward fish. Flotsam and Jetsam, the slimy eels who were Ursula's minions. The mermaid princesses with the *A* names, like Aquata and Arista, including, of course, Ariel.

The only person I didn't see yet was Prince Eric. As I kept munching on my sandwich, I saw the door near the side of the stage open.

The door on the side of the stage opened and a boy walked out, wearing a crown on his head.

The prince.

The boy was running his fingers through his spiky blond hair. He was wearing a white T-shirt and black shorts. I quickly pretended I didn't notice him and focused my attention on punching the straw through my lemonade box. Then I took a big sip. Not noticing him at all.

"Drew!" Flounder yelled out. "Come meet the new dancer, Harper."

Drew.

The prince.

Eric.

The romantic, handsome Drew.

Drew turned to me and let out a big smile. A really nice smile. I nearly choked on my lemonade.

"Hey," Drew said to me. "My name is Drew. Welcome to the ocean."

"Mmm." I knew I was smiling awkwardly.

Then a girl came out onstage.

"That's Ariel," Zora whispered to me. "Her name is legit Ariel. I think her parents knew she was born for this role."

Funny enough, beside her name, Ariel also had reddish-blond hair, which was up in a messy topknot, and I assumed that would be covered by a red wig for her role. She had confidently came out onstage, like a leading lady. She didn't notice me and went right over to sit with Drew onstage. She whispered to him comfortably, and I looked away.

"PEOPLE!" Mrs. Elliott came out onstage, and everyone stopped talking. "I hope you've all met our newest cast member, Harper, who has been kind enough to help us out in our time of great need."

Everyone turned to look at me. I waved shyly.

"Harper is a fabulous dancer," Mrs. Elliott said. "As you'll soon see."

Ariel started waving her hand.

"Can we show her one of our scenes?" she asked. "So she can get an idea of what we're doing? Maybe 'Part of Your World'?"

Everyone agreed with her, including Mrs. Elliott. That was a song Ariel sang, so she'd probably picked it so she could show off to me. I got it. She was the star. I slid off the stage and went to sit in one of the audience seats in the front row to watch it.

Ariel stood alone onstage while Mrs. Elliott cued the music. And she started to sing, "I want to be where the people are. . . ."

This was one of my favorite songs in life, and she was a really good singer. She was onstage alone for only a few seconds when she was joined by Flounder, who harmonized nicely with her. Then almost everyone came onstage—the mermaid world's characters surrounded Ariel, and the human world's surrounded Drew and sang in a big chorus. They all got in a line and did a simple choreographed jazzy box step while they sang. The dancing was kind of a mess, with everyone bumping into one another. The singing was amazing, though.

When it was over, I clapped loudly and everyone bowed and high-fived each other.

"Sorry, sorry, I was off!" Ariel apologized. "I didn't hit that end note."

"Mer-sisters, more arm movement," Mrs. Elliott called out. "Humans, more emotions! Please, everyone, take a seat."

Everyone came down and sat around me. The mer-sisters sat near me grumbling. Ariel came and stopped in front of me.

"We just learned the dance," she said, sounding anxious. "We still have two more weeks until the show to rehearse it. Also, I know I didn't hit that one note."

"You're a great singer," I told her honestly.

"Thanks," she said, smiling. "We're excited you're here! I took a workshop at DanceStarz this summer—it's really intense. You must be really good!"

"Aw, thanks," I said.

"Harper!" Mrs. Elliott called out. "Let's walk you through the routine you'll be in."

I hopped up onstage. She told us that they'd already

rehearsed the dance with the previous dancer, so I was the only one learning it for the first time.

"It's a piece with the underwater cast," Mrs. Elliott. "To the song 'Under the Sea.'"

"Oh, I love that song!" I said happily.

And they taught me the dance.

Sebastian the crab would be singing. Ariel and Flounder would be off standing near stage left, with all of the undersea characters dancing on to the stage, pushing a wheeled platform holding a giant oyster shell.

Then they'd all stop, duck down, the oyster shell would open . . . and inside would be . . .

Me!

"You're the pearl," Ariel called out. "Isn't that cool?"

"Yeah!" I said. "Really cool!"

Everyone seemed to be really happy for me. I sneaked a glance at Drew, and he was smiling and watching my reaction too.

I smiled too. Right back, until I realized he was looking past me toward his other friends. Ugh.

Then Mrs. Elliott walked me through my dance steps.

I would start by doing a waking-up-from-a-shell thing with some flowy moves with my arms, then I would do a leg hold. I'd jump down and would weave between the sea crea-tures, and Ariel and Sebastian. Different characters would do a little dance move with me—Sebastian did a salsa move with his crab hands in the air. The mer-sisters twirled me around. Flounder held his nose and did the swim. Then I did a quick waltz with Sebastian. It was fun and funny.

After, I would go center stage and do a turn series: five pirouettes and a big high kick, ending in a split.

Finally, I would go back into the oyster shell and Ariel and Sebastian would finish the song themselves. It wasn't a crazy-hard dance, but I would have to weave in and out of a lot of people, so timing would be important so we didn't knock anyone down. But mostly, I had my moments to shine in this number, and it was a fun, upbeat dance.

When we were done walking through the moves, Ariel called out to Mrs. Elliott.

"Can Harper show us some of her dancing?" she asked sweetly.

Everyone was like, *Yeah! Show us a dance!* They all went to sit in their seats.

Everyone else in the cast cheered as I went up onstage.

"Okay," I said. "Um."

I decided to shut up and express myself through dance

instead. I took my prep and held my plié for a second, then pulled up, spotting five turns. I nailed my landing and then finished the combination with a big turn sequence across the stage. After my final turn, I struck a pose.

The cast's applause echoed throughout the auditorium.

"Thanks!" I said shyly. I was so into it that when the bell rang and lunch was over it took me a second to remember I was even in school. Everyone jumped up and went to get their stuff to go to their next classes, and some of them waved good-bye to me.

"Harper!" Mrs. Elliott called me over. "Nice job. Are you comfortable with the dance choreography so far?"

"Definitely," I said. "It's a cool routine. I'll practice it at home, too."

"We're happy to have you here," she said.

"I . . ." I smiled. "I feel really welcome here."

"Good. Next practice is Wednesday after school."

And with that, my first official school musical rehearsal was over. And it wasn't as bad as I thought—in fact . . . it was So. Much. Fun.

"nder the sea," I sang under my breath. "Darling, it's better. . . ."

The song had stuck in my head, but it was a happy one. I had Studio D to myself, as I waited for Vanessa to arrive for our first private lesson about my lyrical solo. I did a mermaid-like shimmy. I reached up high and watched myself in the long mirrors. I was wearing a blue-green leotard with sequins around the neckline, inspired by my lunchtime rehearsal "under the sea." I'd been in a good mood the rest of the day, and math and Earth Science had flown by.

When I felt warmed up, I retraced the steps from the dance number, watching myself in the mirror. When it came to the waltz with Sebastian, a different image popped into my mind. It was me, waltzing with Drew instead. I closed my eyes and danced around. I pictured placing my hand on his shoulder, and him taking my hand in his. We would dance around gracefully and—

"Ahem."

I snapped my eyes open. Megan was standing there grinning.

"I didn't hear you come in!" I said.

"Obviously," she said. "Sorry to interrupt your romantic dance."

"I'm . . . I'm," I stammered. "I'm rehearsing."

"Are you doing a waltz in your solo?" Megan asked. "A solo waltz? That's so weird."

"It's not for my solo!" I protested. "It's for—"

I stopped. I didn't want to tell Megan about being in the school musical before I told Vanessa. And I didn't want to give her any more ammunition to use against me as to why she should get the solo instead of me.

"Hey." I changed the topic. "Why are you even here? This is supposed to be my private. Didn't you already have yours?"

We had picked the times earlier for private lessons to learn our solos. I knew Megan had signed up before me.

"Yeah," Megan said. "I did. My dance is awesome. Wait until you see it. Totally a winning solo. The tricks are amazing!"

Now I knew why Megan was here. She wanted to throw me off. I wasn't going to fall for it.

"Good for you," I said calmly. "Are you here to spy on mine?"

"What?" Megan was flustered. "No! No, of course not."

"Then why are you here in my private, Megan?"

"I said I wasn't." She was annoyed now, because I wasn't falling for her tactics.

"Megan, this is Harper's private session." Vanessa walked in, startling both of us. "With me. Do you need something?"

"I just stopped by to . . ." I could see Megan trying to come up with something quickly. ". . . invite Harper to something! A party! No wait, not a party, because no time for parties when we're rehearsing! I meant for fro-yo! Yes! Sugar Plums! For Squad bonding time after this!"

"Squad bonding time sounds good," Vanessa agreed. "Later. Right now, I'd like Harper to be stretching so she can make full use of her private class, just as you did yours."

"Of course! Leaving now! Good-bye!" Megan looked flustered, backing out of the room.

I held in a smile.

"Harper! Let's talk about your solo!" Vanessa said. "I chose lyrical for you because I know you've had some success in the past with it."

I nodded. I had won top junior solo at nationals for my old dance team with a lyrical routine.

"I want to build on that success," Vanessa said. "However, I also believe in challenging yourself and enhancing your skills."

"Last time I did seven pirouettes in my turn series," I reminded her. "Maybe this time I can do eight."

Vanessa nodded thoughtfully. "While that's not a bad idea, I have another one. I don't want you girls to think I'm focusing on your weaknesses and feel self-conscious, but I also know you'll be a stronger dancer if we address them."

"My footwork," I jumped in. "I know, I had problems with my footwork."

Vanessa laughed.

"That's true, you did," she said. "But you worked on that already and had a marvelous improvement. You've shown an excellent work ethic and focus. I'm rewarding that with a dance that I honestly believe is a competition winner. It's challenging—but are you up for the challenge?"

"Yes!" I said. "Definitely!"

"I'm giving you a real opportunity to prove yourself with this," Vanessa said. "I know you have it in you."

That was cool! I was really pumped. She was telling me she had faith in me. She'd noticed my work ethic and my focus! I was all in!

I definitely would not be telling her about my school musical today.

"As you know, the song is called 'Taking the Leap.' Let's listen to the music," Vanessa said.

I sat down on the floor and closed my eyes as the first notes of the song played. I let the music wash over me. A woman began singing about being brave, challenging yourself, doing things that scare you.

When the song ended, I opened my eyes.

"I want you to think about what story you want to tell with that song," Vanessa said. "Take some time and think about it. Let's walk through the moves."

And we did! My favorite part was the turn series. I felt like that showed off my best skills.

After we walked through the steps, I turned to Vanessa. I would start in the center of the room, doing a floating turn into some floor work.

"I really like this routine," I told her. "The opening and how I go high and low throughout."

"Good start," Vanessa said.

"Thank you! I'll go find some studio space now!" I said, already planning on how to practice the turn on my turn board. I got my bag and texted my mom to see if I could stay for Sugar Plums. When I went out, I ran into Lily in the hallway. Her solo private was next.

"How was it?" Lily asked.

"Mostly good," I said. "Hey, I hope yours goes great!"

"Thanks," Lily said. "Hey, did Megan ask if you can meet at Sugar Plums after this?"

"Yeah," I said. "Do you know what that's about?"

"Team bonding," she said. We both looked at each other skeptically. I got a text and checked it to see my mom had said that I could stay later.

"I'm going to practice my new dance," I said. "Meet me after?"

I went to the front desk to see where there was an open studio. Studio E was a small room with mirrors and a barre. There were a couple younger girls in the corner practicing a duet. I said hi to them and found my own corner.

Five, six, seven, eight.

I worked on the steps for the next twenty minutes, watching myself carefully in the mirror. I forgot some of the moves, but I'd only just learned them, so that was okay. Some of the steps I remembered I knew I could do better. I needed to practice my transitioning from that float turn to the floor. I needed to nail my pirouettes and the actual floor work. I'd have to practice a lot more. A lot.

Finally, Lily came in to get me.

"How'd it go?" I asked her.

"Whew," Lily said. "Vanessa threw a lot at me all at once. That was a little scary."

"Yeah, same," I said. I grabbed my duffel bag and pulled on a T-shirt dress over my leotard. I slid on my flip-flops and headed out of the studio.

"Speaking of 'a lot.' I'm a little scared of Megan's idea of team bonding, though. Why does she want to 'bond' all of a sudden conveniently after we get our solo dances?"

I was obviously suspicious of Megan's motives too. Especially after she showed up at my private.

"You know you can trust me," I said. "If you need help or anything, let me know. But I'm thinking I'm going to keep my solo routine a secret from the Bunheads, at least for now."

"Yeah," Lily said. "I was thinking that too."

"Hello, hello!" Lily's dad called out from behind the counter to us. The Bunheads were already sitting at one of the high-top tables. "Harper, did Lily tell you about our new offerings? We are celebrating fall coming, with caramel apple frozen yogurt and candy corn as a new topping."

"I'll try them!" I said, taking a little test cup. It was fun to try the new stuff. I didn't really like the caramel apple fro-yo, but I definitely liked the candy corn. I got a bigger cup and poured myself a mix of vanilla and Creamsicle, and put candy corn and marshmallow fluff on it.

Then I joined everyone at the table. Megan and Riley were drinking smoothies, Trina had a boba tea, and Lily also had a cup of yogurt. I sat down next to Trina, across from Riley and Lily. Megan sat on the end of the table.

"How can you drink that stuff?" Megan was saying to Trina. "The squishy things in it are gross."

"I like the little bubbles," Trina said. "They're so chewy."

"So slimy." Megan rolled her eyes. "Everyone is here. Let's get to business. Let's talk solos. Riley, you start."

"Wait, what are we doing?" I asked. "I thought we were here for team bonding."

"Exactly," Megan said. "I thought we could bond over our solos. Let's go around the table and tell the hardest moves Vanessa gave you. Riley, you go first."

Hmm.

"Well," Riley said. "My hardest move is my aerial. It's hard because—"

"So," Megan interrupted. "Harper, how about your dance?"

Megan wasn't even trying to be subtle. Megan was gathering intel so she could compare our dances.

"I think I need a little solo time with my solo before I share," I said. "To bond with it."

Lily snorted quietly.

"Pfffft!" Megan said. "We're a team. Just tell something."

"Okay," I said. "I really like my dance. It's intense."

"Intense? Intense as in slow and boring? Mine is pretty dramatic and fast-paced and exciting," she boasted.

"I meant intense as in challenging," I said to her. "You know, how Vanessa said she was going to challenge us—"

"What's your hardest dance move?" Megan interrupted me, leaning in.

"I have a couple of them," I told her, taking a casual bite of my yogurt. "What's your hardest dance move?"

"I have a couple of them too," Megan shot back. "More than a couple."

"Yeah," I said, not giving in. "Same."

"Megan, come on," Trina said, rolling her eyes. She turned

to me. "She just wants to know how hard your dance is compared to hers."

"Excuse me!" Megan glared at her.

"That's what you said!" Trina protested.

"You're not supposed to tell them that," Riley hissed, and the table moved. Trina grabbed her leg and winced from the kick under the table.

"Wow, this is great team bonding," Lily said cheerfully.

"Okay, okay," Megan grumbled. "Let's move forward. Next on my agenda—"

"You have an agenda?" I asked her.

"Yes," Megan said. "Since Vanessa refuses to choose an official team captain, I'd like to propose that we have an unofficial one."

"That is a great idea," Riley said, sounding very rehearsed. "I nominate Megan. All in favor, say yes."

"Um, what even is happening here?" Lily looked at me.

"Wait a minute," I said. "We haven't discussed this. What does a team captain do?"

"A team captain is the captain, the leader, the person that leads," Megan explained slowly, like I was a little kid.

"Yeah, I get that," I said, suspiciously. "Specifically, though. What would you do?"

"Well, they have . . . really good ideas, okay?" Megan said. "And it's easier to run things if you have a captain. I mean, seriously, haven't you had captains on your teams before?"

"Sure, for my lacrosse team," Lily said.

"Well, there you go," Riley said. "Okay, let's try again with nominations."

Megan's eyes nearly bulged out of her head at that as she stared down Riley.

"I nominate Megan—again." Riley picked up on her cue.

"I nominate Harper," Lily said.

That was really nice of her. But it was obvious we were outnumbered by Bunheads.

"I still don't think this is legit," I said.

"Let's vote!" Megan said. "Everyone who thinks this is legit, raise your hands."

Megan and Riley raised their hands, and Trina raised both hands.

"You can only vote once," Riley said to Trina.

"I know, but Megan said to raise your hands," Trina told her.

"Three to two. We are going to vote on a captain," Megan said. "Okay, everyone who votes for me, Megan, to be captain, raise one of your hands."

Riley and Trina each raised a hand. Megan jumped up and clapped.

"Oh my gosh, thank you all!" Megan clasped her hands to her chest. "I'm honored to be your captain. Your fearless leader."

Lily looked at me. I shrugged back. I wasn't too worried about this. Megan always tried to take charge anyway, so until Vanessa told me Megan was the actual captain, I didn't know if anything changed.

"So, Madame President, what will be your first order of business?" I asked her. Her face lit up. She was really taking this seriously.

"Well, since some people aren't willing to be team players with solos"—Megan gave me a side eye—"let's discuss the group dance."

That actually sounded like a good plan.

"Well, we all agree we want to step up our game," she said. "So I looked at all our class schedules and came up with these times for additional rehearsals."

Megan sent out a group text. I skimmed it. Monday after rehearsal, Tuesday after class, Wednesday before class . . . Whoa. She had us scheduled every single day plus weekends.

There was no way I could do this. Especially now that I was

going to be in rehearsal in the school musical on the weekends.

"Um, I'm not going to be able to do this schedule," I said. "School stuff."

"Me neither," Lily said. "I have to help at the store."

Megan leaned on the table with her hands.

"Third place," she said quietly. "Who here is happy with third place?"

"Top three was good for our first competition," Trina protested.

"Not! Good! Enough!" Megan pounded the table with her fists, making us all jump, including the family sitting a few tables down.

"Is everything fine over there?" Lily's dad even noticed. "Can I get you something? A relaxing lavender tea?"

"We're fine." Lily smiled at him.

"Mr. Sugar Plums," Megan said. "Would Lily be able to rehearse a little more the next few weeks until our next competition? After that, we can offer you extra help. Riley here will help out any way she can!"

Judging by her face, this was news to Riley.

"Well, we're hiring someone new," Lily's father said. "So Lily will have extra time."

"I will?" Lily brightened. "Oh, cool! Thanks, Dad!"

"Well, that's exciting," I told Lily. She seemed really happy.

"So we're all good!" Megan said, totally disregarding me.

"Uh . . ." I raised my hand. "Not quite. I'm going to have to miss a couple of these."

"I'm not going to apologize for being passionate about this. I want us to be champions," Megan said. "Did you see what the Bells posted?"

I hadn't. I did look as Megan held up her phone.

The Bells' new team, Energii, was standing in their white, yellow, and orange team jackets. Isabella was front and center in the picture, holding a huge trophy.

"What's that from?" Trina gasped.

"They went to Alabama for a competition," Megan said. "They posted that last night. They came in first place. First!"

"Energii is really good." Trina nodded. "They've gotten lots of first places."

"Yes, but hello? Who's holding that first-place trophy? Isabella," Megan said. "It's the Bells' first win there—and they're letting Isabella hold the trophy like she won it for them."

Megan looked at each of us fiercely.

"Don't you want to post a picture of the Squad with a first-place trophy?"

Yes, I could totally agree with that one. No-brainer. I

wasn't going to let Megan push me around. We all knew she wasn't *really* the captain. But she did have a point. We did have a lot of competition, and we did want to win. In her own way, Megan was motivating. Annoying, but motivating.

"First! Place! Trophy!" Megan said, waving the phone in my face. "Harper, it's all up to you now. Are you in?"

Everyone looked at me.

"I'm in," I said. "DanceStarz on three!"

We all put our hands in, went *one, two, three*, and cheered!

"This is going to be the best dance ever," Megan said.

*T*his is going to be the worst dance ever!" Zora said, too loudly. Mrs. Elliott turned to her and Zora looked at us sheepishly.

"Please show a little faith," Mrs. Elliott said. "We are improving every—NO! Eeels! NO! Left, right, through—not under!"

Rehearsals for *The Little Mermaid* dance were actually going really well—for me! My dance steps were tricky, but nothing compared to what I had to do for competition dance, so I felt my confidence rising every time I was onstage with the others.

But overall, the dance wasn't going so well.

"Crabs! Crabs scuttle forward-back-forward, not back-forward-back!" Mrs. Elliott called out.

"Sorry!" One of the seaweeds stepped on my foot. "Sorry!"

"It's okay," I told her. It was, except when we tried it again, the seaweeds were a beat late and almost knocked a puffer fish off the stage.

"Okay, let's break on 'Under the Sea' for today," Mrs. Elliott said. "Why don't you all head to your regular lunch. Chef Louis, stay behind to work on the kitchen scene."

I went down the steps off the stage and grabbed my stuff.

"I can't get that timing to work," Courtney the eel complained. "I keep knocking into the mer-sisters."

"We noticed" Zora sighed.

"I think you're moving too early. You need to move on four count, not three," I suggested, tentatively.

"I have no clue what that means," Courtney said.

"On the combo? The eight count?" I continued. Courtney just shrugged.

"I've never taken a dance class in my life."

"Me either," Frankie said. "Dancing is really hard!"

"Tell me about it!" I laughed. We reached the cafeteria and I said good-bye. I went over to sit with Lily, Riley, and Naima.

"Oh!" Lily perked up. "I thought you weren't going to be here today. Because of your . . . um . . . quiz."

She looked over at Riley and Naima, but they weren't really paying any attention anyway.

I really needed to tell Vanessa about my musical so I could stop hiding it.

"I finished my quiz early," I said. Just as I sat down, Zora and Courtney came up to our table.

"Hi, Pearl!" they said.

"Who's Pearl?" Riley looked around.

"Sorry to bug you, Pearl," Zora said. "But can you explain what you were talking about with the eels, the crabs, and the mermaids? We're kind of stressed."

Riley leaned closer to me.

"Uh, we have a science quiz," I said to Riley. "About sea creatures."

"Mermaids are on your science quiz?" Riley asked us.

"Ha!" I let out a little nervous laughter. "Ha-ha! Mermaids on a science quiz!"

I realized I was coming off like a total goof. Riley was looking at me, eyebrow raised.

"I'll be right back!" I said cheerfully. I jumped up and fled across the cafeteria to a table that was full of the cast and crew eating their lunches.

"Harper's going to help us with our dance," Zora announced.

"Hey, Harper!" "Pearl's here!" Everyone shifted down the bench to make room for me. Ariel, the girl playing Ariel patted the seat next to her. Prince Eric was sitting down the table, on the other side. I felt a little shy as I sat down with them.

Drew. He was cute.

"So, Harper." Ariel turned to me. "Your dancing is amazing. Teach me your ways."

"Oh!" I smiled at her. "Thanks! You're already a good dancer, though—and singer."

"Have you seen her act, yet?" Zora said. "She's a triple threat. Do you act and sing?"

"I definitely don't sing. My little sister has a good voice, but not me." Then I paused and surprised myself by saying: "I kind of would like to act a little, though."

"You can try out for the spring play!" Ariel said. Everyone else nodded. It was nice how enthusiastic and supportive they all were.

"Oh wait, I don't know about that," I said, quickly changing the subject. Acting seemed pretty scary. It was the one part of dancing I was really trying to improve. "But anyway, did you have dance questions?"

"Oh my gosh, yes," Courtney said. "I keep running into everyone."

"She does." Frankie nodded.

I thought about how the dance had gone. While I'd been concentrating on trying to do my best, I also had noticed what was going on around me.

"Okay, one issue that you guys are having is your timing." They looked at me blankly. I stood up and pushed back my chair. "Okay, let me demonstrate."

I went in front and showed them a simple combo they had, going by counts. One, two, three . . . I danced as everyone was craning their necks to see what I was doing.

"I can't see! Can you do that again down here, too?" someone down the table asked.

I waltzed down the length of the table, then I added a little spin. I smiled when I saw people nodding, like they were getting what I was trying to say. But then my smile dropped. I could see Riley watching me from across the cafeteria, very interested.

"You know what," I said. "Maybe I can go over this later, at the next rehearsal? I mean, if it's okay with Mrs. Elliott. She's the choreographer."

"Oh, she'd be thrilled," Ariel said. "She has to work with us on so many things. Maybe we can meet after school or over the weekend?"

Ouch—that would be kind of hard because of this whole rehearse-every-day mission Megan was on. I was about to say I couldn't, but then—

"Pearl?"

I looked up behind me. Drew was standing there. His dark blond curls flopped over his head as he looked down, and he smoothed them back with his hand.

"Would you help me with my dancing too?" he asked.

"Yar," I said stupidly. "I mean, yes! Okay! Yes!"

Oh my gosh, now I was sounding like a super dork. He probably regretted even asking me.

"Please, please help us." Ariel laughed. "When we do our last dance together, it's so awkward. Last time we did our waltz, I practically punched him in the face. By accident, I swear!"

"And I stomped on her foot." Drew laughed.

"How about Saturday at my house?" Ariel said. "We have a big basement, and I can invite everyone."

"Great, I'll be there!" Drew said.

"Me too!" I said, a little too enthusiastically. Fortunately, he didn't pick up on that.

The bell went off. Oh my gosh, I hadn't even started eating my lunch. Everyone started packing up their stuff to get ready to leave.

"Bye, Pearl!" Ariel said. "See you Saturday!"

"See you Saturday!"

'm starving!" I said as I burst into my house. "Feed me!"

"We have to leave in forty-five minutes!" Mom said.

I looked in the fridge. I grabbed some cheese wedges and strawberries. I was so hungry, I immediately stuffed some berries in my mouth. Mo was jumping around my feet, hoping to catch some people-food crumbs. Then I went to the pantry and opened the door and—

"AAAAAAHHHHHH!" I screamed. Something grabbed my leg.

Hailey was scrunched up in the bottom of the pantry.

"Ha!" Hailey jumped out of the pantry, holding my mom's video camera. "Gross, you just spit berries all over me."

"Well, guess what? I wasn't expecting you in the pantry," I told her, wiping my mouth off.

Mo barked around us.

"It's for *Hailey on the Daily*! I'm doing pranks."

"Okay, no," I said. "Give me that camera."

"Don't erase it!" Hailey said. "Don't erase it! I need material!"

"Give me the camera or I'm telling Mom," I said. Hailey made a face and gave me the camera.

I rewound her camera and watched what she'd been filming. I watched as Hailey's face came on-screen.

"I'm hiding in the pantry," Hailey whispered. "My sister will be coming home from school, and she always gets a snack. I'm going to freak her out. Okay, I hear her! She's coming!

Then the screen gets light as I open the door and then . . .

Mmflpmp.

You can hear me scream, but you can't see anything except Hailey's floral leggings. Then you can hear Hailey say, "Gross, you just spit berries all over me!"

"How'd it come out?" Hailey asked me. "How's it look?"

"Well," I said, "I think you need to work on your camera skills a little."

I handed her the camera, and she watched it herself.

"Oh, no! You can't see anything!" she wailed. "That would

have been so good! Now I have nothing for today's show!"

"Sorry," I said. "It's not like you're really posting daily, so nobody will really know."

Her face fell.

"Hailey, I think you're taking this too seriously," I said.

"But it's called *Hailey on the Daily* for a reason. Will you help me film something else today?" Hailey asked.

"I have to eat and get to dance class," I said.

"Come on, Harper. I have to sit around and wait at your studio for your class tonight, so I won't have any other time." Hailey kept on asking.

"Sorry," I said. Then I realized I was going to ask my mom and Hailey to stay even longer, so I could do the group rehearsal Megan set up, and I felt bad. "All right, let's film something quick. How about we do something with no prep. Weird facts tag?"

This was something I'd seen online that looked kind of fun. I pulled up the questions on the kitchen tablet and angled it on the counter so we could read it.

"Okay." Hailey shrugged, setting up her camera on its little tripod feet. "That works."

"Hey, I'm here from *Hailey on the Daily*, and today we're doing . . ."

"Weird facts tag!" we both said into the camera.

"Nobody really tagged us, but I'm making Harper do it anyway," Hailey said. She read off the questions.

"'Number one: What's a nickname only your family calls you?'"

"Harper-roo," I said.

"And we call you Harper-potamous," Hailey said, cracking up.

"Nobody calls me that," I protested.

"'Number two: What's a weird habit of yours?'"

"Hair twirling," I answered. "It drives my mom crazy when I twist my hair."

"'Number three: Do you have any weird phobias?'"

"Arachnophobia," I said, shuddering. "Fear of spiders. That's so legit me. I have this fear of waking up at night and a tarantula is crawling on my face."

"Ack!" Hailey shrieked a little. "Gross."

"I know," I said.

"'Number four: What's one of your biggest pet peeves?'"

"When you're eating and the fork scrapes your plate." I cringed. It made me hurt just thinking about it.

"'Number five: What's one of your nervous habits?'"

"Biting my nails."

"'Number six: What side of the bed do you sleep on?'"

"So in my old bedroom I slept on the right side of the bed," I said. "But here in Florida, I sleep on the left side."

"'Number seven: What was your first stuffed animal and what was its name?'"

"A teddy bear named Teddy?" I couldn't really remember.

"'Number eight: Do you have any weird body skills?'"

"My thumb is double-jointed!" I held up my finger to the camera. "Look, I can bend it weird."

"'Number nine: What's your favorite comfort food?'"

"Frosted cereal flakes. Oh, and mini chocolate chip muffins. Yum," I said. I wondered if there were any mini muffins left.

"'Number ten: What did you used to wear that you thought was so cool, and now you don't?'"

"I used to think all my outfits were pretty cool," I laughed. "I literally wore pink sparkly tank tops with matching skirts and matching shoes with a headband. I was so extra!"

"And that's Harper's ten weird facts!" Hailey said. She ran over to turn the camera off.

"That went pretty well, right?" I asked her.

"Yup!" she said. "Thanks!"

"Harper!" My mom walked into the kitchen. "Are you ready?"

"Oh, no!" I looked at my phone. It was time to leave for dance! I stuffed two of the cheese wedges I'd gotten out earlier in my face, but was still starving, so I ran back to the pantry and grabbed a pack of mini muffins. Then I ran to my room to get my dance bag ready. When we got in the car to go to dance rehearsal, I settled in the front seat and opened the muffins. Hailey was already in the backseat with headphones on, car dancing in her seat.

"That was very nice of you to spend time with your sister," Mom said. "I know you're busy."

"Mmmf," I said, with my mouth full of muffin.

"How was play practice today?"

I swallowed my muffin.

"It was good!" I said. "We rehearsed the dance, and I got it almost right away. Then I had lunch with the cast and they asked me to help them with their dance moves. Oh! Is it okay if I go over to Ariel's—that's the girl who plays Ariel—house Saturday to teach the people some dance technique? Some of them have never taken dance before!"

"Sure," my mom said. "I'm happy to hear you're meeting some people at school."

"Yeah, they were nice," I told her. "So in my dance, I'm surrounded by ocean creatures, and I get to pop out of a giant oyster! So everyone's calling me Pearl—how cute is that?"

"Very cute," Mom agreed. "And Vanessa said the schedule works out with your dance team?"

I obviously hadn't told my mom that I hadn't told Vanessa.

"Oh, sure. I'm sure it will work out." It was all working out so far. There was probably no reason to make her think I wasn't focused.

"And your grades?" Mom asked. "Are you keeping up your grades?"

"I got an A on my math quiz," I told her proudly. *Just don't ask about how my book report is going and we'll be just fine!* I'd get it done, though. I leaned back, a little stressed out now. I had to finish that book report, and then I had a science quiz—a real one, not a fake one—coming up and—

"Harper, please don't twist your hair," my mother said. "It drives me crazy."

CHAPTER

The next day, I realized I hadn't told Mom about the extra practices Captain Megan had now declared mandatory. After dance class, I went to the lobby to check with Mom. She was on the couch with Megan's and Riley's moms. My mom wanted me to make more friends in our town—but I knew she wanted to make some too. She was getting to know the dance parents, but Lily's parents were always at the shop. So it was mostly Megan's and Riley's moms she got to talk to at the studio. Those two had been best friends since forever.

But this time, she was sitting off to the side on a bench with my sister and neither of them looked happy.

"Noooooo," Hailey groaned. "Quinn's in ballet, and I'm sooo bored."

"Your sister was 'soooo bored,' she decided to hide behind the couch and secretly film me talking to the other mothers," my mother said. "So we are ready to go."

"But, Mom," I said, "Megan is seriously on this mission, and I can't be the only one to miss it. Can Dad pick me up after?"

"Honey, your father is working really late," she said. "You'll have to tell Megan no."

I texted Megan:

Hey, sorry, Mom needs to leave with Hailey. Can't make it. 😣

She was not going to be happy.

"I need to go apologize to the other mothers, and then we'll leave." My mom sighed. "Harper, please watch your sister."

I turned to my sister.

"Thanks a lot," I snapped. I saw Megan quickly coming into the lobby and spotting us. "Oh great, here comes Megan. Now I have to hear about how I have to miss important practice."

"Hi, Megan!" Hailey brightened up. Little kids loved Megan, for some reason.

"Aw, look how cute your pigtails are," Megan said sweetly to Hailey. She turned to me. "So, wait, you have to go?"

"Yeah," Hailey said. "I got in trouble for filming the moms. They were talking about getting new curtains, so it was not even worth it."

"Oh, really?" Megan looked like she was trying not to laugh.

"Yeah, I've been taping for my new channel," Hailey continued. "*Hailey on the Daily*, soon to be an Internet sensation as soon as my mom lets me post things, in like a zillion years."

"Hey, do you want to shoot a video for me?" Megan asked her. "I mean, for the Squad? Of our routine?"

"Sure!" Hailey said. "I mean, I'm not a professional or anything."

"That's okay—it's just for us to watch," Megan said. "You can capture our mistakes so we can critique them later."

"Cool!" Hailey said happily.

"Oh wait, you have to leave," Megan said. "We were going to rehearse, but—"

"Let's ask my Mom!" Hailey grabbed Megan's arm. Not that I particularly wanted my little sister following me around "capturing my mistakes." However, I saw where Megan was going with this, and it was kind of genius. While Hailey dragged Megan over to the moms, I followed.

"MOM!" Hailey practically jumped on my mom. "We have to stay! I'm going to film! I need the video camera back!"

"Excuse me," my mom said to the other moms. Then she turned to Hailey. "As we discussed—"

"I'm sorry about filming you!" Hailey said to the other moms on the couch. "I just thought you'd be interesting!"

"She means like a documentary on the interesting lives of moms," Megan saved her. "She thought you had star quality."

"Oh!" Megan's mom bought it. "That's so sweet. Really, no apology necessary."

"Mrs. McCoy." Megan turned to my mom sweetly. "I hope it's no trouble, but Hailey could really help out the Squad rehearsal if she could stay and film our routine."

"Please!" Hailey begged, dancing around her.

"It would be great if I could rehearse," I added.

"Fine," my mother said. She handed Hailey the video camera. "Use this for good, not evil."

"Yay!" Hailey said. She grabbed Megan's hand. "Let's do this!"

I had to give her credit, she was taking charge of this. And when we ran through our group dance, Megan also remained in charge.

"Five, six, seven, eight . . . ," she counted off, and we danced.

Hailey filmed quietly, running around us but surprisingly not interfering.

"All right," Megan announced. "Let's watch it."

Hailey propped up the camera on the table, and we all crowded in to watch on the screen.

"Agh, I hate watching myself back," Lily said. She half covered her eyes.

"It's so awkward," Trina agreed.

"So cringey. It's like you zoom in on anything you do and think it's bad." I said. I hated watching my footwork, my leg extensions weren't high enough, I felt like I didn't draw the eye like Riley did, and—

"But that's the point!" Megan said. "Because we want to step it up or we're not going to get first place. So here are my suggestions. Our timing is off, our spacing is bad, half of you have dead face, and people aren't pointing their feet."

"Gee," I said. "Is that all?"

Everyone started protesting.

"I thought you guys were great!" Hailey said loudly.

"Well, thank you," I told her, suddenly appreciating having my little sister in the room.

"But sometimes boring." Hailey added on that last statement unexpectedly.

"Hey!" I said.

"Wait, we don't we don't want to be boring!" Riley said.

Which was true. We needed to capture the audience's—and judges'—attention.

"This is something I was thinking. We have to have a serious discussion," Megan said. "How can we make this routine more exciting?"

"Shouldn't we ask Vanessa?" Trina asked.

"Yes," Megan agreed. "But I think she'd be open to our ideas. We all know we're not doing everything we can with this dance. Riley, we need to kill your solo combo."

Nobody was expecting that.

"Wait. What?" Riley said. "WHAT? Kill my solo?!"

"Hailey." I gestured for her to leave the room. I didn't want her to see what might happen. Fortunately, Hailey didn't seem to want to see it either. She shot me a scared expression and ran out of the room.

"Sorry, yes," Megan said, without flinching. "We need to go back to plan B, what we did in the competition. The turn series–kick over."

The turn series–kick over was something I'd invented at the last minute.

At our first competition, Megan had stepped on Riley's

hand, and we'd had to change the choreography. Riley and Megan's partner tricks and Riley's hand-walking had to be switched out.

And that's when I had my shining moment: I got to do a really cool turn series. Two pirouettes, a kick spin, and then Megan leapt at me, sliding forward under my leg and daringly melting down into a hinge. I twirled over her and she popped up and then ducked down as I twirled over her.

I'd promised Riley when her hand healed, we'd go back to the original. So we had. Part of me was relieved, because our substitution was really hard and really risky. One miss in timing, and I'd kick Megan in the face or fall over on top of her.

"So we want to win," Megan said. "What's our most impressive trick? It's the partner trick that me and Harper did. Riley, we have to cut your hand-walking. It's not that great. The replacement combination was better."

"What?!" Riley said. "Oh, fine. That is a cool combo. I'll do it."

"I didn't mean you would do it," Megan said. "I meant Harper would do it. Again."

Riley gave me a side eye.

"I don't know," I told Megan. "I don't want to take away from Riley—"

"What do you mean 'take away from Riley'? How about *giving* Riley something—a win!" Megan shouted. She went up to Riley and started shaking her hand like she had a bell in it. "Do you want the Bells to think they did the right thing changing studios? Do you want them to beat us again?"

"No," Riley said. "But I want a solo—"

"Sorry!" Megan said. "The best people for it are me and Harper. Harper can pirouette, and she has the timing. We need to do that."

"But we did that move last time and we didn't win," Riley protested.

"And you had a busted hand in it," Megan said. "And we hadn't rehearsed that, which screwed us up. Now everything can be perfect. With the new moves, not yours."

"Oh, come on! Who made you boss?!" Riley said.

"You did," Lily and I both said.

"You did vote her captain," Trina pointed out.

"I take back my vote," Riley said. "I'm voting for Trina."

"Yay!" Trina said happily. "I got a vote!"

"Well, we have to ask Vanessa anyway before we make any changes to the routine," I said. Plus, part of me was secretly hoping she'd say no. I had enough going on without having to worry about doing this move again.

"I want to bring her a united front," Megan said. "Everyone in favor of asking Vanessa if we can have the best routine for the competition, raise your hand."

Everyone raised their hands. Even Riley grudgingly did too.

"That means we'll tell Vanessa we all—and I mean *all*—think Harper and I should do the partner trick," Megan said. "I'll go see if Vanessa's around."

She ran out the door. We stood there in silence. Riley sat down on the floor and glared at me.

"Personally, I think Vanessa is going to say no," I said. "If that makes you feel any better, Riley."

"And you still get to do your hand-walking, which is really cool," Lily said.

Vanessa walked in the room.

"I hear you're doing extra rehearsing on your group dance," Vanessa said. "I'm pleased to hear this. Megan says you had a few concerns."

"We want to step it up, up our game, go for the win," Megan said. "May we use the same routine we did in competition, with Harper and me doing the partner trick?"

"Hmm," Vanessa said. "It definitely was an impressive move that caught the judges' eyes. However, it's a risky one. Is everyone on board with this?"

"Yes," all of us answered, three of us confidently. Riley and I glanced at each other. For once, we were on the same page. Hesitant.

"Harper and I will rehearse it like crazy," Megan promised.

"That sounds fine," Vanessa said. "I'll want you to set up some more one-on-ones with me or one of the assistant coaches. Carry on."

More privates? I barely had time for this. I had an inner freak-out as Vanessa left the room.

"Yess." Megan jumped around. "Woo! I talked her into it! Seriously, aren't you all glad I'm captain? What are we all standing around here for? Let's get practicing! Chop chop! Harper! Get your sister back in to film again."

Sigh. Megan was on a serious adrenaline rush and power trip. I went out into the hallway to get Hailey. Hailey happily came back in. Megan put on our music, and we all got in formation.

Lily ran over by me.

"Psst," she whispered. "Congratulations! I think? How do you feel about this?"

"I . . ." I was about to whisper something back, but remembered Hailey had the camera. I forced a smile on my face. "I feel great!"

"Five, six, seven, eight . . . !" Megan yelled.

We ran through the dance one more time.

"Sloppy!" Megan yelled. "We're not in unison! Again!"

"Again?" we all groaned.

"Picture that platinum number one trophy in my hands," Megan said. "I mean, our hands. All over social media, everyone liking it and the Bells being super jealous. This is our motivation to win!"

"I'm kind of tired," Trina said. "I already did lyrical class today, you know. And I taught some little kids to do their heel stretch turns before that."

"Five, six, seven, eight . . . !" Megan called out. And we did the dance again.

First, Trina wobbled on a leap. Then, Lily missed a count. And when Megan and I did the partner trick, she slid toward me. I kicked over her, and that part went totally fine, but then she scowled at me—so when I went to do the leg hold at the end, I wobbled over her. And fell on her.

"OUCH!" Megan yelped and rolled out from under me. "What is everyone's issue?!"

I rolled over too, on my back on the floor. I lay there panting.

"Megan, you're wearing us out," I said.

"Then we need to run through ag—"

"Oh, look at the time. I have to go to my acro class!" Lily interrupted her. "Yikes, I'm going to be exhausted for it."

"Fine," Megan said. "Next priority, apparently, is building stamina. See you all tomorrow. And the next day. And the next—"

"I think we created a monster," I grumbled to Lily as we walked out the door.

"We didn't vote for her for captain," Lily said. "It's Riley and Trina's fault."

"My bad." Riley was standing outside the door, and had overheard us. "I didn't know she was going to take away my partner trick with her. And replace me with you."

"Trust me, I'm not entirely thrilled either," I said.

"Harper!" Megan stuck her head outside the door. "You can't go yet! Let's set up our sessions with Vanessa now! Partner trick, you and me!"

Definitely not thrilled at all.

After meeting up with the other girls, we went to Squad rehearsal, already exhausted from Megan's rehearsal.

Vanessa stood at the front of the room.

"You've all been working hard on your dances," Vanessa said sternly. "But has it been hard enough?"

Lily and I exchanged glances. Inwardly, I groaned. She was going to make us work even harder? The Bunheads were sitting on the studio floor next to us, looking just as frustrated.

"The answer is yes! You have been working hard enough,"

Vanessa said, unexpectedly smiling. "So today we're going to take a little break and choose your solo costumes!"

COSTUMES!

"Yay!" we all cheered with relief—and excitement.

"I've been waiting for this moment!" Riley yelled. Riley wanted to be a fashion designer, and she was always eager to see the costumes. She was probably going to have her own line of dance costumes someday.

Vanessa opened a cupboard door and pointed to a shelf of catalogs.

"Help yourselves," she said. "Each of you select two or three options, and we'll review them together."

We each grabbed some catalogs and spread them out on the floor. Vanessa told us what our budget was and to be sure to pick costumes that fit our category of dance.

"I've never gotten to choose my own costume before," Lily said. Lily had only gone to a ballet school before DanceStarz, so she was particularly excited about having more options. Ballet outfits were so pretty and there were so many choices, but I could tell Lily wanted something totally different from the classic ballet look. She flipped right to the modern, sleek designs that would be great for tumbling.

I could pretty much choose anything for a lyrical routine, but since my song was slower and flowy, I decided I'd pick something flowy too. Hmm.

"How am I going to decide?" Trina said. "There are so many pretty ones!"

"I know," I said. I looked at all the color names: turquoise, violet, burgundy, evergreen.

"I want them all," Megan said, then wrinkled her face. "Ew, except that one."

I looked over her shoulder to see a neon orange–colored dress that did look . . . unfortunate. We all cracked up.

"Your moms were talking about their worst costumes," I said to Megan and Riley. "I guess they thought one looked like a chicken."

"The worst costume I ever had was as a flower," Trina said. "I was really excited until they put a flowerpot on my head as a headpiece."

We all cracked up.

"I wore a bodysuit that went from my feet to my head," Riley said. "It looked like I was a pink sausage."

"I wore a leotard that was supposed to be green but turned out to look like someone puked on me," I said.

"Now you guys are making me a little happier I only did ballet." Lily laughed. "Although some of my Nutcracker costumes were a little weird, they weren't that bad."

"Every costume looks good on me," Megan said. We all groaned, and she grinned.

"Okay, I think I found my costume!" Riley announced. She held up a page with a dramatic white dress with a one-shoulder top and a silver sequined skirt.

"Hmm. I was planning to wear white," Megan said.

"Oh," Riley said and paused. "Maybe I should wear something brighter for jazz, anyway. Probably like red."

Megan nodded, satisfied.

Riley lived to please Megan. I sighed. I considered choosing a white dress for myself, but I wasn't going to be like that. Also, I didn't want to wear white.

"Okay, I got mine!" Megan announced. We all turned to her, but then she said, "No, no, maybe not good enough."

I flipped through the dresses. I thought about what Vanessa had said, about choosing the outfit to match your song.

"So hard to choose," I said.

"Well, what's the name of your song, again?" Trina asked.

"'Taking the Leap,'" I said.

"I found one for you," Megan said. She slid a catalog over to me. "Number three."

"The green one?" I grimaced. It was dark green with neon green stripes.

"Yeah, taking the leap," Megan said, and laughed. "Like a frog."

I tossed the catalog back at her.

"I found my choices," Trina said. "I always get put in pretty light pink costumes. SO, for my tap I'm going with my signature pink costume, but . . . here's my favorite."

She held up a page with a fuschia sequined tuxedo-style jacket, over a black leotard. With black tap shoes, it would look really striking.

"I like that!" I said.

"Riley?" Trina turned toward Riley, who perked up. Riley liked that we knew she was our fashion person. "What do you think?"

"This is a bold choice, and you know I like that," Riley said. "It will pop onstage."

"You should wear these tights with it," added Megan.

"Oh, I think that would make it too costumey," Riley said. "I think just simple black."

"Riley, can you help me with my outfit?" Lily asked.

Riley beamed and Megan scowled. I knew Megan liked to be the expert in everything. She was super stylish herself, but Riley just had a way of being trendy and a little unique at the same time. I actually admired both of their styles, although they were different from mine.

Riley leaned over Lily's catalogs and poked her finger at a page.

"Do you like that?" Riley asked.

"'Copper,'" Lily read. "Huh, I never thought of that color."

Riley showed us the page. It was a shimmery copper crop top with copper-and-white striped briefs.

"I think a metallic would look sharp!" Riley said enthusiastically. "Like a flame, whipping around the stage. With a high pony and a cool hair clip!"

She flipped through another catalog and found what she was looking for.

"That's really cool," I agreed.

"And totally different from a ballet costume," Lily said happily. "I like it! Thanks, Riley! I'll look for something for my hair."

"Okay, okay, I think I have mine," Megan said. Everyone turned their attention toward her. "No, wait, it's not good enough."

We all went back to our catalogs. Riley announced she had made her top choice. It was a multicolored dress in deep red, purple, and emerald jewel tones, covered in sequins. We all told her that would be perfect for jazz.

Megan and I were still flipping through pages, with nothing to show.

"Why is this so hard?" I complained. I felt overwhelmed. I wanted to find the perfect one.

"I know," Megan said quietly. I nodded in solidarity with her. Flip, flip, flip.

Yellow? Gray? Floral? I kind of liked a floral leotard, but it wasn't really me.

Megan scooted a little closer to Riley and paused on a page. Riley looked over her shoulder and gasped.

"That's gorgeous," Riley had barely said when Megan grabbed it back and held it up.

"Here's mine!"

It was a white cold-shoulder turtleneck with lace blocking on the waist, which flowed out into a mesh skirt. The entire thing was covered in shining white sequins, small and large.

"Wow," we all said. It *was* gorgeous.

"That's not in the budget," Riley noticed.

"My mother will take care of it," Megan snapped the catalog shut confidently.

It was gorgeous. I knew my parents would never let me go over budget, so I wouldn't have as many luxury options. But seriously, there were still so many I could pick that I liked! I sighed. I was the only one who hadn't picked one. I had found some ideas—about fifteen of them. They were all lighter-colored with dresses or skirts. I was surrounded by open catalogs, each dress pretty but not feeling exactly right.

"I need help," I announced. Everyone scrambled around me. "I like this look, but nothing stands out."

"Okay, that gives a good overview. How do you want to feel when you're dancing?" Riley asked.

"Like you're about to lose to me," Megan snarked. Everyone looked to see my reaction, but it was kind of funny, so I just laughed.

"No, that's not what I'm going for," I said. I thought about it. "My dance is really soft and dreamy. That's why I was thinking a dress—"

"And your favorite color is purple," Riley remembered. She reached over and grabbed a catalog from her own stack. "I might have seen something in this catalog that had some fresh ideas."

She flipped through the catalog and stopped on a page. Riley handed it to me.

Ooh. I read the description out loud.

"An orchid mesh crop top with mesh insets . . . Oh, I haven't done mesh before," I said. "And a mesh skirt. Riley, it's so different, but I love it."

I held it closer to Lily for her opinion.

"That's so pretty!" Lily said.

"It's going to float around you when you do your turn series," Riley said. "But it's light enough it won't trip you up."

I glanced at Megan, waiting for another snarky remark about tripping up. But she surprised me.

"Oh, that's cool," Megan said. "Yeah, that's a good one."

"You guys," I said. "We are going to look so good."

Everyone smiled at each other. We had a moment of team bonding. But it didn't last long.

"Well, don't get too excited," Megan said. "Only one of us is going to dance a solo."

"So does that mean only that person gets to actually get her costume?" Lily asked.

We all froze.

"Vanessa wouldn't get us all excited to pick a costume for no reason." Trina worried. "Would she?"

"Yes," Megan said confidently. "Do you really think she's going to get us all a costume and only person gets to wear it? She probably had us pick to motivate us to try harder."

Hmm. We fell silent, as we realized we'd never thought about that strategy. Would Vanessa really do that?

It sounded like she would.

10

It was already Saturday, and it was time to go to Ariel's house for our *Little Mermaid* "rehearsal." Luckily, Ariel lived close enough for me to ride my bike over. I checked the directions on my phone, grabbed my helmet, and then rolled my bike down the driveway. It felt like forever since I'd ridden my bike, and I actually wobbled when I got on it at first.

I rode down the sidewalks, passing the other one-story houses on my street. I waved to two little kids who were drawing in chalk on a driveway. I turned the corner and rode down a hill. I swerved to the right to avoid running into a boy skating on a longboard. As I passed him, I heard him call out to me.

"Hey, Pearl! I mean, Harper!"

It was Prince Eric! I mean, Drew!

"Hi, Prince Eric! I mean, Drew!" I half skidded to a stop.

"Hey." He skated up to where I was.

I smiled awkwardly at him. He was wearing a gray T-shirt and black shorts and sneakers.

"Are you going to Ariel's?" he asked.

"Yeah." I nodded. Yup. Yes, I was.

"Cool, want to walk together?" he asked me.

"Yeah." I nodded again. Okay, could I say anything other than *yeah*?

AUGH! I was acting like a goof. I could feel my face was red, and I pretended to concentrate on wheeling my bike.

"So, is this your first play?" he asked me.

"Yeah," I said, then caught myself. "Well, first legit play. In second grade I was in a food pyramid skit. I played a potato."

"A potato?" He laughed.

"My costume was a giant brown paper bag stuffed with . . ." I realized I was sounding weird. "Anyway, have you been in a lot of plays?"

"Literally never," he said. "I tried out for this one thinking I wouldn't even get a part. It's crazy."

"Wow, and you got the lead," I said. We walked kind of

slowly, me balancing my bike and his carrying his board. I focused on trying not trip over the bike, fall over the bike, or run him over with the bike. "Do you like it?"

"It's fun," he said. "But . . . it's hard. There's a lot of lines to memorize, and the dancing is really hard. I don't know how you remember all those steps. That's really cool."

"Oh," I said. "Thanks! Well, I've had a million lessons since I was three. So maybe I can help people a little. Anyway, I can't skateboard at all."

"It's awesome once you get the hang of it," he said. "It's like you're flying."

"I feel like that when I do leaps and jumps," I said. I smiled. I felt like this conversation was going way better than I would have thought. He was really easy to talk to.

"I'm just learning jumps on my board," he said.

"Like what?" I asked him.

He put the board down on the ground and pushed off. He rode for a little bit, then he kicked it so it flew up a little and he landed.

"That was cool!" I called out.

Then he sped up and kicked out again. I opened my mouth to cheer for him, but then the skateboard slid out under his feet. He stumbled and fell on the ground, on his back. His skateboard went flying ahead, up the street.

"Uh," I coughed. "Are you okay."

"I'm good, I'm good," he said. He ran after his skateboard and grabbed it. I hurried to catch up with him. That was awkward. I didn't want him to be embarrassed, but I didn't know what to say. I guess he didn't either. We walked the rest of the way in silence. Fortunately, it was only a couple more minutes until we got to Ariel's house. While I was pulling my bike up to the garage to park it, he ran ahead to the front door. Ariel opened it, and Drew went in quickly, before I even made it up the front steps.

"Hi!" Ariel waited for me, holding open the door. "Everyone's downstairs. We're so happy you're here. You should have seen us dance at rehearsal last night. We desperately need you."

"Oh." She was so nice. "I'm sure you're fine without me."

"Mrs. Elliott is great," Ariel said. "But I think she's almost given up on our dance."

I followed Ariel through her kitchen, and she introduced me to her father, who was friendly too. We went downstairs to the basement, where a bunch of people were playing foosball and pool, or hanging out on the big comfy-looking orange and teal couches. There was a long table with a lot of snacks on it. The basement was huge!

"This is great," I said, looking around.

"Thanks," she said. "We moved some stuff out of the way so we could rehearse in here. Do you want some food?"

"Get your food and come here, Pearl!" Zora called out from a couch.

I got a paper plate and put some doughnut holes and some popcorn on it. I glanced over to look for Drew, and he was playing foosball with some people. I went over to sit with Zora, Courtney, and a seaweed, who introduced herself as Marlee.

"So, how did you become such a great dancer, and why haven't you been in any of our plays?" Zora wasted no time putting me on the hot seat.

"I started taking dance when I was three," I said. "So I had to at least be decent after all of that time, right?"

Everyone laughed.

"And I just moved here from Connecticut, which is why I haven't done any of the musicals," I said. "Plus, I've never been in a play before, because I take dance five or six days a week."

"I take dance!" Marlee said. "Only once a week, though. My parents said it's expensive."

"Yeah," I said. I was lucky and grateful I could take so many dance classes. "Where do you take it?"

"At Energii," she said.

"With the Bells?" I blurted out, and wasn't sure if I sounded weird about that. "I mean, we competed against them and that's who I met from there."

"Isabella and Bella?" Marlee said. "Yeah, they're new on the ultimate team. I don't compete, so they've never talked to me. They're really good, though."

"I took ballet when I was in preschool," Frankie said. "My mom says I was the first kid to ever fail out. I just lay on the floor in class every day."

Everyone laughed.

"She's the best clarinet in marching band, though," Zora said. "And she's in Robotics Club. And Courtney's on crew."

"You could join," Courtney, who played Jetsam, said. "We need coordinated people on the river. You have to get there at six a.m., though. Then in the spring I do field hockey."

"Wow, you guys do a lot," I said.

They laughed.

"A lot? You should see what Ariel does," Seaweed said. "Basketball cheer, model United Nations, and she's starring in the play!"

"What? Are you talking about me?" Ariel came over, smiling.

"Yeah, about all of your clubs," Zora said.

"That reminds me, I'm co-starting an Environment Club,

and we're doing a park cleanup Tuesday afternoon if any of you can come," Ariel said. "But for now, we should practice the dance moves. Harper, are you ready?"

"Definitely," I said, standing up. "I was starting to feel kind of inferior to all of you talented people."

"What? It's *your* talent we need here," Ariel said.

Everyone moved to the empty part of the basement and got in formation. It looked like everyone in the basement was in this dance. Ariel pulled out her phone and turned on some music. The finale song came out all over the room. They walked through the steps, in time with the music. Ariel introduced King Triton to Prince Eric, and then everyone came out to dance with them, getting into couples and doing a waltz around Ariel and Drew in a big circle.

Then they all paused, and Drew put a ring on Ariel's finger. Then they leaned in—for the kiss? Okay, I have to admit that I got very distracted. Thoughts raced quickly through my head. Was Ariel was going to kiss him, like in the movie? That would be weird, having to kiss someone onstage. I don't know if I'd want to do that!

But, if I did, I'd probably okay with it being Drew. Ack! My face turned red. Then I started to look away so I didn't have to watch them kiss. But I didn't have to worry.

Drew swung Ariel out into a twirl. There was no kiss. Ha! I laughed out loud.

Then they grasped hands and began to waltz in a circle, with the rest of everyone. It was lovely, until—well, Drew missed a count and sailed into another waltzing couple.

"Oaf!" It was like a domino effect. All the waltzers knocked into each other.

"Okay, okay, stop!" someone else said. The music stopped.

"See the problem?" Zora said. "We're always running into one another."

"Ham," I said. "What does Mrs. Elliott say?"

"She says things like, watch your footwork," Scuttle said. "But I tried to watch my feet and I practically smacked my partner in the face."

"That's true," his partner said, and everyone laughed.

"Mrs. Elliott makes me nervous," Courtney said. I noticed a lot of people nodding.

"Yeah, if we can fix this, she'll be really happy with us," Ariel said.

"Maybe we if try it slowly," I said. They tried again. "Eight counts . . . one, two, three! Four five six . . . !"

Yeah, their timing was WAY off. There were too many couples trying to keep up, and trying to be on the same beat.

Hey, I'd been there. When I first tried to learn the Squad's group routine, it had been way faster than I'd been used to, and I couldn't keep up. This routine was far slower and, to be honest, seemed pretty easy to me. For a minute, I wasn't sure if I could teach something that came so naturally to me.

But I'd been dancing since forever. They hadn't. And I thought about what had helped me in that instance.

Or rather, who.

Trina had a special way with teaching footwork and timing. Vanessa had her teaching some of the Tiny Team and beginners, and when I couldn't master the footwork, she had asked Trina to help me. Trina was an understanding teacher.

I should ask Trina if she can help. I was confident she could really help them out.

Then I realized why that probably wasn't a good idea. I hadn't told anyone other than Lily that I was even dancing in the school musical. If I told Trina, then the Bunheads would find out, and Vanessa would find out. I just had to hold on a little longer until Vanessa assigned the solo. So no.

"Harper," Drew said. "Can you help us?"

He looked at me, and his hair flopped over his eye so adorably. So yes.

I could ask Trina not to tell anybody yet. Trina took pride in not embarrassing anyone who needed help, and hadn't told anyone that Vanessa had asked her to help me last time. That was nice of her.

"I have an idea," I told them.

*T*rina said yes! Yes, she would help *The Little Mermaid* cast with dancing, and yes, she would keep it totally a secret.

I had told Lily, though. I didn't want her to think I was keeping secrets from her again. I'd even invited her to come with us. Everyone was going to meet at Ariel's house later that evening.

But first I had to go to a semiprivate lesson. Megan and I were going to work on our partner trick with Vanessa. I walked into the studio and passed Trina with the Bunheads on the way to her class.

"Harper!" Trina whispered loudly. Then she gave me a huge wink.

Subtle, Trina.

Megan gave her an odd look, but didn't say anything.

"Harper!" she said urgently. "Are you focused? We need to get this down perfect, you know."

"I know." It came out more like a sigh than I'd expected it to.

"TBH," Megan said, "I'm not really so excited about this either."

"It was your idea," I said, going into the studio.

"Actually, I was going to try to come up with a cool trick for me and Riley to do instead," Megan said. "But after that last competition I realized Riley cracks under pressure, so what could I do? Wait a second. You don't crack under pressure, do you?"

"No," I said firmly. Then I went to the barre and began doing stretches. Megan joined me a few feet away.

"Good, because wait until you see what I'm thinking," Megan said. "You can handle a few new tricks, right?"

"Uh, yeah?" I said. "Depending on—"

"Hello!" Vanessa came in. "Megan, you told me earlier you had some ideas. I'm open to hearing them."

"I was thinking that Harper does two more turns over me and then I do a side split while she does an aerial."

Wait, what?

"That sounds a bit ambitious," Vanessa said.

"Harper said she's up for the tricks," Megan said, shooting me a side eye.

Vanessa looked at me. While I had technically said that I was up for a few new tricks, Megan hadn't specifically said which ones.

An aerial? That was crazy hard for me, especially after I'd already been twirling. I could completely get knocked off my feet on that one. I was still working on perfecting my aerials.

"Have you rehearsed this?" Vanessa asked.

"Not yet. I thought we could try it here first," Megan said.

"Okay," Vanessa said. "Let's do it. Start at the combination before. Five, six, seven, eight . . ."

I had no idea how this was going to go. I took my prep and went through the first eight counts. Then Megan and I ran to the center of the room near each other and did the initial partner trick. One, two, three, four—I managed to get my two spins in and kick over her, but this time, having to add on the aerial threw me off, and I stumbled a bit, adding two extra steps.

Meanwhile, Megan was doing her little side split, and she looked fantastic.

"Megan, very nice. Just watch that arm. Harper, no, no,

watch your timing. I want to see you hit the floor on five," Vanessa said, "or you're going to be off balance every time. You might even run into Megan, and we don't want that. Let's try that again."

Megan looked at me and shrugged.

Hmm.

We went through the routine again, and pretty much the same thing happened. I couldn't get it together. And not just the new move—I was messing up the simple step combos, too. I glanced over at Vanessa's face, and she looked concerned.

"While I'm pleased to see you both taking on a challenge, I'm afraid I can't approve these moves for a competition," Vanessa said. "It's too much."

"Hmm," Megan said, obviously disappointed. "I'm sorry. I thought it would work. Harper is usually so good at turn series."

Excuse me?

"We'll just go back to the partner trick we did at the comp." Megan sighed. "I'm sorry we disappointed you."

"You didn't disappoint me, Megan," Vanessa said.

I looked at Megan. I could see she was holding back a smile, and I realized my hunch was right. Megan hadn't disappointed Vanessa—but maybe I had. Megan had set me up to fail and herself to look good. I squinted my eyes and gave Megan a look. She widened her eyes and smiled back innocently.

"Vanessa, maybe we can at least add an aerial to my solo?" Megan asked.

"How about you work on your current partner trick and see if we can get that solidified first," Vanessa said. "Five, six, seven, eight—"

I was off my game the rest of the lesson. Any time Megan came near me, smiling, I got mad. I was mad at her for trying to make me look bad, and at myself for actually looking bad.

"Kick higher, Harper!" Vanessa called out. "Turn quicker on the second count—"

When our half hour was up, I was so ready to be done.

"Thank you, Vanessa!" Megan said. "That was awesome!"

Yeah, awesome. For her.

"I love your striped top!" Trina's sister, Alexis, said, as I climbed into the passenger seat of her white car. I'd started to sit in the back, but she and Trina had insisted I sit up front.

"You're our guest!" Trina said cheerfully.

"You're the ones doing me a favor, though," I reminded them. "Thanks again, Trina, for helping teach. And Alexis for driving us."

"So why I am driving you to whose house?" Alexis asked me.

"Ariel's," I said. "She's a girl in my grade who's playing Ariel in *The Little Mermaid*. They're having problems with the group dances. Some people haven't ever taken dance before."

"Oh, that happens in cheer sometimes," Alexis said. She was the cheer captain at her school. "Hey, I teach the dance moves for our freshman tryouts. Do you want me to come in and help too?"

"Oh, I don't want to bother you—" I said.

"It would be fun!" she said. Trina was nodding.

"It's, um"—I paused—"kind of a secret from everyone at DanceStarz that I'm doing this. I, um, don't want to embarrass the cast."

"No worries," Alexis said.

We pulled up to Ariel's house, and I remembered the last time I walked up here with Drew. I hadn't seen him, except once in the halls when we both said hi. They'd been rehearsing other scenes, not the one I was in. I felt a little left out, so I was excited to be part of things again. We rang the doorbell, and when Ariel's father answered, I introduced her to Trina and Alexis.

"I was told this was a special occasion that required special snacks," her father said. "So make sure you try the tot-chos. It's a tater-tots-and-nachos mash-up."

"Dad . . ." Ariel came into the kitchen. "Let them go. Quick, escape him."

"Oh, my feelings." Her father clutched his heart. "The pain!"

They both cracked up.

"Actually, tot-chos sound awesome, thanks," I said, and Trina and Alexis nodded.

"Hey, everyone!" Ariel yelled out. "Harper's here!"

"Hi!" I called out. Everyone said hi, and I realized Ariel was waiting for me to introduce Trina and her sister.

"So, this is Trina," I said. "She's on my dance team, and she's a really good teacher. She made my dancing so much better."

"Aw, thanks." Trina smiled.

"And her sister, Alexis, who is captain of West High's cheer-leading squad!" I said. I punched my fist in the air, and then realized that looked kind of dumb, not spirit-y.

"Oh, cool!" Everyone looked super impressed.

"We can show you our hardest dance, the finale," Ariel said. Everyone gathered in the middle of the basement, in their waltzing duos and their little huddles of sea creatures and humans. Then music began, and they all started dancing.

The dance went well for the first few minutes, but then the same thing as before happened. Someone missed a step, the timing went off, and people knocked into one another. Trina and Alexis jumped right in to help. Trina immediately took Zora and her urchins off to the side. Alexis worked with the bigger group.

I smiled. I watched for a few minutes. Then I had really nothing to do, so I went to the table that had the snacks. Mm. Ariel's father really had gone all out on those. I made myself a plate with some cheddar chips, a mini chocolate chip cookie, and yes, some tot-chos. I watched the dance, munching. I felt mostly happy, but a little left out in a way. It was hard for me to watch a fun dance and not want to jump in myself.

But—OKAY—I also especially may have been watching a certain prince. He danced with Ariel, twirling her around and then moving around in a circle as he reached out to the other dancers, who danced around them.

"All right, I see a major problem," Alexis said. "Everyone come over here. I mean everyone!"

I got up and joined everyone over toward her.

"Let's try this in small groups," Alexis called out. "Humans and Ariel, stay with me! Everyone else can sit out."

The sea creatures all went straight to the snack table. Zora came over with a bowl full of BBQ chips first.

"Wow, that really helped," Zora said. "Trina broke down the steps into mini steps for me, so I actually understood."

"She has a gift for that." I nodded.

"Those sisters are amazing," Flounder said, coming over with an overflowing plate. "Also amazing are the tot-chos."

They were really good. I took a big bite of tot-chos, just as I heard Alexis call my name.

"Harper! I need you to dance with Drew!"

I nearly choked on my tot-chos.

"Ack!" I coughed.

Zora pounded me on the back, until I stopped coughing. I thanked her with a wave, and stood up. *Pull yourself together, Harper,* I told myself. I cleared my throat and went over to Alexis and Trina, who were standing with Scuttle, King Triton, and Drew.

"Okay, so we are going to waltz to show them the footwork Trina taught them," Alexis said. "Harper, just stay on the beat, and twirl on five. Partner up."

Alexis held her arms up to King Triton. Trina held her arms out to Scuttle.

And Drew held his arms out to me. *Gulp.* I had to hold his hand and then put my other hand on his shoulder.

I hoped my hands weren't sweaty.

"Sorry if my hands are sweaty," Drew said, as if he were reading my mind.

"You're good," I squeaked. Okay, at least if we were sweaty he'd think it was him.

"When your left foot goes forward, Prince, Harper's right

foot will be going backward," Alexis explained. "One, two, three, and one, two, three—okay, freeze. Down, up, up, and . . ."

Drew stepped on my foot.

"Sorry, sorry," he said. I could see he was legit embarrassed.

"Don't worry about it," I said. "I get stepped on all the time. And worse—one time I basically kicked my dance partner in the head."

He cracked a small smile. We all started dancing again, and this time Scuttle and Trina came too close to us.

"Okay, Scuttle is stepping too wide." Alexis was calling out directions so we didn't step on our partners or run into one another. "One, two, three! Rotate, two, three!"

We awkwardly moved around. I noticed what was going wrong. He noticed me noticing.

"I know, I stink," he said.

"No, no," I reassured him. "It's just . . . you keep pausing before you turn, and then you're off a half beat."

"Just push me where I should go," he said.

Okay. I took the lead on the dance, and kind of pushed him so he could get the timing right.

"Just don't overthink it," I told him, giving him advice my dance teacher told me for years and years. "Just relax and one, two, THREE!"

We danced around a little bit.

"Hey, okay, better, right?" Drew said, sounding relieved when I nodded. He grinned at me. I grinned at him.

"Looking good, Drew and Harper!" Alexis called out.

And that's when we realized the music had stopped. Everyone else had stopped dancing. Except the two of us.

Uh. We immediately stopped and dropped each other's hands. I was about to be super embarrassed, but he leaned into me.

"Thanks," he said. "That was cool."

Eee.

"Erk," I said, my face turning probably purple. I apparently lost my ability to speak.

I raced off to the snack table and grabbed some water.

"Okay, what's the most important thing to remember about dance?" Trina called out.

"Your timing!" "Foot counts!" people yelled. You could tell they'd been listening to Trina.

"NO," Trina said. "Dancing is fun."

Alexis said something to Ariel, who turned on some new music that wasn't from the show. It was a new song I'd just put on my playlist. Ariel dimmed the lights, and it was suddenly like a dance party.

Everyone started dancing around silly, laughing and having fun. I danced around in a little circle with Zora and some of the seaweeds. Then I danced with Ariel and Trina. Then I spun around and found myself dancing with Drew. This time, we were being awkward on purpose.

It was fun.

"uess what?" Lily said excitedly. "My dad hired someone for the store! Finally, one of my parents will be
home, and I can have someone over. Can you come over this
weekend and swim?"

We were standing in the dance studio hallway. I was heading into my private lesson with Vanessa to practice my solo.
Megan was in with Vanessa now. Lily had finished hers before
Megan, and we'd agreed to meet up to hang out. If ten minutes
in a hallway could count as "hanging out."

"Oh, that sounds so fun," I said. I thought about how fun
it was to go over to her house and swim. Back home, summer
was totally over, but here, even though it was fall, it was still

hot enough in Florida to swim. Lily had these mermaid tails we could wear and—wait! Mermaids!

"Actually, sorry, I can't," I groaned. "I have *Little Mermaid* rehearsal on both days. There's only two weeks until the musical."

"But aren't you only in one dance?" Lily asked.

"Yeah." I nodded. I didn't have to be there for every rehearsal, but I'd found that when I didn't go I felt left out. I really liked being a part of that. "But I've ended up helping with all of the dances. It feels like I can be helpful when I'm around. Even Mrs. Elliott asked me if I could come. How cool is that?"

"Cool," Lily said.

"Plus," I said, "it's nice to be there, so it's like I'm part of the whole thing. I really like them."

"Ah," Lily said. "Yeah, it would be nice to be part of that."

"I have to tell Vanessa about it today," I said. "I'm running out of time. I thought maybe we'd know who got the solo by now, you know?"

"But I feel like we have no time together at all. I feel like I never see you anymore," Lily complained. "Just to hang out, not in dance class or without the team."

"Trust me, I know," I said.

"Okay, how about going to Sugar Plums?" she asked hopefully.

"I want to say yes, but"—I sighed—"along with play rehearsal, Megan has me booked on our partner trick both Saturday and Sunday with Vanessa or somebody. Ughhhh."

"Ugh," Lily said.

"I know, right?" I said. "I wish Megan had picked someone else for this. Be glad it wasn't you."

"Wellll," Lily said flatly. "I don't know about that."

When Lily looked away, I realized I'd said something dumb.

"I mean, I'm happy for you that you're getting all of these parts. You get to be in the school musical with no audition! Megan and Vanessa picked you to do the partner trick for our group dance. I know you're stressing. It's just, other people don't get those opportunities," Lily blurted.

She was right. And she was upset.

"I—" I wanted to explain, but the studio door opened.

"You're up!" Megan said. "Harper, I love your leo."

"Thanks!" I said. I was wearing a long-sleeved leotard for the first time. Even though the days were hot, Florida nights were starting to get a little chilly. It was one of my favorites: purple and hot pink block stripes with a high V neckline.

"So, Vanessa wants to talk to us," Megan said, gesturing me toward the door. "I mean me and Harper. Not you, Lily."

Oof. Bad timing.

"Mm-hmm," Lily said.

"I'm sorry," I said to Lily, but she had already turned to go down the hallway.

As Megan and I walked in, I felt awful about Lily. And now I had to focus again in that room with Vanessa, even though my mind was not really here.

"How are you guys feeling?" Vanessa said.

Awful, I thought. But out loud, I said, "I think we are feeling good!"

Megan quickly chimed in, "Yeah! We really want this to work," she declared.

Vanessa nodded, looking pleased.

"If you're both that motivated, I'll let you set up some more lessons. Then I'll touch base with you next week and we can decide if you're going to use this combination."

"Okay!" said Megan.

Vanessa checked her schedule. I could do two of the times she suggested—but the other two I had play rehearsal.

"I have school stuff," I said. "Sorry."

"Oh, Harper," Megan said. "Between this and the solo, I think we need to be more dedicated."

I could tell that "we" really meant "me." And I hated that she was trying to make me look bad again.

"I *am* dedicated," I said. "And I have a private lesson right now with Vanessa, so there you go."

"Yes, you do," Vanessa said. "Harper, why don't you and Megan coordinate schedules later so we can get started."

"I'm always available for dance. I'm going to go practice my aerials!" Megan said, cheerfully as she left.

Vanessa turned toward me.

"How are you feeling about your solo?" she asked.

"I love it," I said truthfully. The song was really pretty, and it had some of my favorite turns in it. Honestly, when Vanessa said she was going to throw in one of our challenges, I'd thought she'd toss in quick footwork or flexibility tricks I had a hard time with. This routine seemed made for me.

"Let's see it," Vanessa said. She turned on my song.

I took my prep and waited for the count. And, go! One, two, three, four . . . I turned! I spun! I leapt across the floor. I reached toward the sky. I spun on the floor. Bam. Bam. Bam. I swung out into a full pose and waited.

Nailed it!

I looked at Vanessa's face, expecting her to look impressed, but she had a pretty blank expression on her face. Hmm.

"How did you feel?" she asked.

"How did I feel about it? Good? I remembered the routine, I got the timing down, I think my turn series were good, and I landed that leap. My triple pirouette into a split was on point, I thought. So . . . good," I said.

"I didn't ask how you feel *about it*," Vanessa said. "I asked how you felt. Technically, you were good. However, I didn't get any emotion from you."

I opened my mouth to protest, but then quickly closed it. I kind of knew she was right. I'd had that feedback before:

"Connect to your audience, Harper."

"Tell the story, Harper."

"Let's see your facials, Harper."

My teachers back in Connecticut had said those things too. I sighed.

"As you know, a dancer who doesn't express her emotions doesn't connect with the audience," Vanessa said. "And if we're looking at selecting a solo for a competition, we would need to make sure you connect with the audience. Including the judges. We want to see things."

I nodded.

"I'll work on that," I said, nodding. I wanted her to know I would take it seriously. I really would.

"How?" Vanessa asked.

"Um," I said. Then I felt my face crumple. "I don't know."

"What did you think when I told you that?"

"I thought how many times I've heard that before," I said. "My teachers have told me that. I don't know how to do it."

"You seem upset," Vanessa said.

"Yeah," I said. "I feel like when I'm dancing I'm putting it all out there and then everyone's like, *Nope. We can't connect to you.*"

I looked down at the floor. I felt pretty stupid.

"I hate to say it, but you're expressing your emotions," Vanessa said. "Tell me what you're feeling now."

"Frustrated," I admitted. "Hopeless."

"You're feeling emotions," Vanessa said. "I can see it. You're connecting with me. So, see, you're not hopeless."

I cracked a small smile.

"Well, let's see if we can finally figure that out." Vanessa smiled. "Let's think about the lyrics. Tell me, what do the words of the song mean?"

"Well," I said. "It's called 'Taking the Leap.' It's about someone who is going to do something new and they're scared of it.

But they just have to get ready and then go for it."

"That's a good analytic answer," Vanessa said, and I smiled. "If you were in English class."

Oh.

"But this is dance class. So let's try answering: What does this song mean to you? Let's see if you can connect to the lyrics," Vanessa said.

She went over and turned off the lights and told me to lie down on the floor and close my eyes.

I lay on the floor. I felt silly with Vanessa watching me.

"I'm not going to watch you. I'm going to leave the room and let you process," Vanessa said. "I'll stand outside the door so you don't have to worry about anyone walking in. I don't want you to move, just lie there."

"Just lie there and . . . ?" I asked her.

"Focus on the lyrics. You told me what story the singer told. Think about how to make it your own. How are you going to tell the story? Do you have your own story you can tell?"

Okay. When Vanessa left the room, she started the song. I lay there in the dark, listening to the music. I'd heard the song lots of times, obviously, since I'd been practicing the dance. *Take the leap, don't hold back. Blah blah, I got it. Try something new, push yourself. Yeah, yeah.*

Hadn't I tried enough new lately? Hadn't I pushed myself enough lately? Yes! I had a story! A new state, a new house, a new dance studio.

I'd leapt! I'd been leaping!

But why didn't I feel like it was enough?

"All right, let's try it again," Vanessa said, returning to the studio. "Pop up."

I jumped up off the floor and took my prep. The music came on. *Tell my story. Okay, arms, tell my story. Legs, tell it.* My facials felt like they were right. I made a confident smirk. I made sure to make eye contact with Vanessa like I would with the judges and then to the sky, like I was connecting with the music. When I turned into my split, I landed perfectly. Ta-da!

I looked at Vanessa for validation.

"Well, you projected emotion," Vanessa began. "But the emotion felt tense. I couldn't relax watching you. Harper, you need to get out of your own head."

I couldn't help it. I let out a sigh.

"I know you're trying," Vanessa said. "Look, you've got what some people consider the hardest part down! Your technique is excellent. But there is more to dance than just great technique. Be vulnerable. Put yourself out there. Think of your character."

Vanessa paused. "Harper, have you ever done any acting?"

14

"Acting?" Zora said, clapping her hands. "Of course I'll help you!"

"I feel kind of silly, but . . . ," I said, looking around as if someone was going to spy on me. We were walking down the hall, heading to lunch.

"Silly?" Zora said. "Did you think we were silly when we asked you for help dancing?"

"No," I admitted. "Okay."

I'd decided to ask Zora, because she was the most outgoing and, to be honest, the loudest. I figured if Vanessa wanted me to put myself out there, Zora was the person who put herself out there the most.

"Actually, I'm flattered," she said. "But you should ask Ariel, too. She's the lead. And she's really nice."

"Oh, I know she's really . . . nice," I faltered.

"Does she make you feel intimidated?" Zora knew what I was thinking. "I know she seems intense, but she's good at that stuff too. I can ask her for you. I mean, more teachers, more ideas."

"Okay," I agreed. "That's true."

We went into the cafeteria. I told her I'd see her later, and went to sit with Lily, Riley, and Naima. They were already eating their lunches.

"Ask Harper—she was there." Riley and Naima were laughing. Lily rolled her eyes at me.

I sat down next to Naima.

"How was your Spanish quiz?" I asked Lily. I'd seen her stressed-out post about it last night.

"It was—" Lily started to tell me, but was interrupted.

"Harper!" Zora and Ariel came up, holding their lunch trays. "Mrs. Elliott said we could use the arts room. Let's go!"

"Uh." I looked at Lily. I didn't know they would want to help me now.

"You're helping them again?" Riley raised an eyebrow. "Are they at least paying you?"

"Sorry, I have to go," I said, mainly to Lily. I jumped up and quickly shoved my stuff back into my lunch box. Then I lowered my voice and whispered to Lily, "Sorry."

Lily slumped down and didn't respond. I felt bad leaving her, but I had to get out of there before Riley got suspicious. I began to follow Zora and Ariel out when Zora turned around.

"Can we stop at my locker really quick?" Zora asked. We headed toward her locker upstairs. While Zora grabbed what she needed, I filled them both in.

"It's kind of weird to think people are watching my face and my feelings so much," I confessed. "I wish they'd just focus on my dance technique."

"Ha!" Zora said. "I wish people would just focus on my face and not my dancing. I'm totally extra with my faces. In drama class, Mrs. Elliott is like, *Be subtle!* But as Zora, I get to go big."

Zora made a few faces. She was definitely expressive and animated. She opened the door to the arts room and—

OH! A bunch of drama people were in there. Flounder, Frankie, and Courtney and the other sea creatures. I did notice Eric/Drew wasn't in there, to my relief.

"I kind of thought it was just us," I whispered to Zora. "This is so embarrassing."

"Oh, I'm sorry!" Zora covered her mouth. "Everyone

wanted to help you, like you helped all of us. The 'humans' are rehearsing with Mrs. Elliott, but the rest of us are here!"

"Was it embarrassing when we asked you for help with dancing?" Ariel apparently had heard me. "I hope not! Now it's our turn."

Everyone smiled at me.

"Okay, so we thought you could do your dance and we'd try to guess the story," Zora said. "We do this in class with improv. Like charades."

Everyone nodded.

"I mean, it's not like it's a play. I'm not a character with lines or anything. But . . ." I gave in. "Oh, okay. Should I play the music?"

"No," Zora said firmly. "No clues. Just you."

I took my prep and then . . . I danced. With everyone watching me, I made an extra effort to do my facials and express myself with my body. When I finished, everyone clapped.

"You're an amazing dancer!" Zora said.

"Aw. Thanks." I smiled.

"Let's see if you told your story. What emotions did you see?" Zora said. Some people raised their hands, like we were in class. "Sebastian?"

"You're stressed out," Sebastian said. "You have a big test or something to go through."

"Um," I said. "I start stressed out, I guess, but then . . . ?"

"Then nothing?" Sebastian shrugged. "You still seemed stressed out."

The whole time? Ugh.

"I think she seemed worried," one of the ensemble members said. "Then something happened during her twirls where she's about to let loose. But then she has to jump over something scary and then she dies."

"She dies?" I squeaked. "It looked like I died?"

I looked over at Ariel. She shrugged.

"I wouldn't say died," she said. "More like, faded away."

"Yeah, she didn't have enough emotion for a death," Courtney agreed.

People started shouting out adjectives.

"Serious!" "Intense!" "Bothered!" "Frustrated!"

"All right, all right!" I finally had it. "Didn't anyone see me change halfway through? I was stressed and frustrated at first? But then hopeful and determined? Then finally, triumphant?"

Silence. Nothing.

"Seriously?" I asked. "I reached like I was longing for

something? No? Then I landed the leap like I reached my goal?"

Everyone was looking around, at the floor, anywhere but at me.

"I've won major awards for my dancing, you know," I grumbled.

"Nobody's saying you're not an awesome dancer," Ariel said quickly. "We just couldn't understand the story."

I knew they were trying to be nice, but I felt really embarrassed. I felt ridiculous for even coming to a group of actors and trying to act.

All of a sudden, people started yelling out words again.

"Embarrassed! Silly! Ridiculous!"

"Is that true, Harper?" Zora asked. "Are you feeling those emotions?"

"Uh, yeah," I said, confused.

Everyone started clapping. What was going on?

"You're doing it! You're telling your emotions!" Zora yelled and everyone cheered

"Yay?" I said. Everyone cheered, and I said it louder and more confident this time. "Yay!"

"And now you've gone from tentative to triumphant," Zora said, sounding kind of triumphant herself.

"Just like my dance," I said, nodding. "I get it."

"So now, remember those feelings," Zora said. "Use them in your dance."

"Also, see your face?" Courtney came running up with her phone in hand. Ugh! She'd taken pictures of my face while I'd been dancing. I could see the difference in my stressed, tight face versus my "triumphant" face at the end.

"You should have someone tape your faces while you're dancing so you can see when you go out of character," Courtney suggested.

"So embarrassing," I groaned.

"Mrs. Elliott says there's no such thing as embarrassing when you're learning to act!" Ariel said. "You have to put it all out there."

"I'll show you embarrassing! Just watch me even attempt to do that dance you did. Ha!" Zora said.

"Let's do it!" Ariel said. "Okay, everyone! Let's do Harper's dance!"

"Huh?" everyone said.

"You heard her!" Zora said. "We're all going to do Harper's dance."

"Uh, I can't even twirl once," Courtney said.

"I didn't say do it well." Zora laughed. "Everybody up.

Okay, Harper, walk us through the dance and tell us what's going on."

I stood up.

"Take your prep like this." I stood in my initial position. Everyone tried to pose like me.

"All right, what's happening in the dance?"

"She's scared and stressed—" I said.

"She?" Ariel asked.

"I mean me." I realized my mistake. I had to be the character. "I'm scared and stressed."

"Well, you're acting out that part right," Flounder yelled out, and everyone laughed. He was right: My face was definitely stressed.

"So am I!" Courtney said. "I'm scared of these dance moves!"

Everyone laughed more. Especially me.

"Then you do this combination. . . ." I went through my next combination. Everyone around me tried to follow along. Nobody could, and they all started to laugh. Then I walked them through the rest of the dance. One, two, three, four . . . one, two, three, four. When it came to the more complicated holds, everyone tried but fell. The funniest was when I did my turn series and everyone totally fell over into one another. By the time I got to the end, where I leapt, everyone had either given up or just jumped in place, laughing.

"And . . . pose!" I held my pose.

"Yeah, we're totally embarrassing!" Ariel said. I was laughing hilariously, until I saw something that completely threw me off.

"Hey, you're showing your emotions on your face!" Zora said to me happily. Then she frowned. "Uh-oh. And they don't look like happy ones."

Riley was standing at the back of the room. And she definitely did not have happy emotions on her face either.

CHAPTER

15

$\mathcal{I}$ walked into Squad rehearsal, nervous. I hadn't seen
Riley since I'd spotted her in the back of the arts room
earlier that day. She'd left as soon as I saw her.

Maybe she hadn't seen anything. Maybe she wouldn't say
anything.

I entered Studio 3, and the Bunheads were already there.
Riley stood there, her arms crossed accusingly. Trina looked
confused.

"Harper!" Megan smiled. "Hiiiii!"

"Hey," I said. I didn't flinch, as I went to put my bag in a
cubby. Then I sat on the floor to start stretching.

"As team captain, I feel obligated to let Vanessa know if

there's a question of commitment that's affecting the team—we need to take care of it. It has come to my attention that someone has a conflict with an activity that's not dance."

Riley and Megan looked smugly at me.

"ALL RIGHT!" Trina burst out. "I'll tell you!"

Everyone swung around to look at her.

"I joined the Robotics Club!" Trina wailed.

Everyone paused. That was unexpected.

"Robotics? Like, robots?" Riley stood up and did the robot to demonstrate. Then she smirked.

"I know, it's so nerdy," Trina wailed. "But I don't care if you think I'm a big dork!"

"What? I don't think that," Megan said. "Robotics is pretty cool. Really smart."

"Oh!" Trina calmed down a little. "Okay. So anyway, I'm helping program a robot to break down dance steps."

"But it's not cool that you're keeping secrets from me." Megan frowned. "I mean us. I didn't even know you were into robots."

"I didn't either! But I was talking to this girl Frankie when I went to help Harper and her cast. She told me about Robotics Club."

My heart sank.

"You knew about Harper's musical? You helped the cast?" Megan said.

"Oh!" Trina clamped her hands over her mouth. "Sorry, that was supposed to be a secret."

"So many secrets around here," Megan commented.

I cringed. She was really furious. I tried to help Trina out.

"You know Trina teaches people and she has to keep it on the down low."

"Actually," Megan said. "Riley told us about what is going on."

Well, then.

"Okay," I said snippily. "I didn't know I had to report everything I did to you Bunheads."

"You do if it affects us," Megan snapped back. "As team captain, I feel like I need to be apprised when one of us on the Squad goes out of bounds."

Out of bounds? Seriously?

"I saw you showing your dance to a bunch of randoms at lunch," Riley said. "And they were giving you ideas of how to do better."

"So, why would you ask some randoms to help you?" Megan said, circling me. "It's a mystery. That's when I realized what was really going on."

Yup. She knew.

"Spit it out, Megan," I said. She was enjoying stressing me out too much.

"They weren't some randoms! They were professional dance teachers you hired to come in at lunch," Megan finished. She gave me a smug look.

I burst out laughing. "Wait, what?" I blurted. "You think I hired ten people to teach me?"

"You probably need a lot of help." Megan shrugged. "So you didn't hire them?"

I shook my head. I couldn't believe my secret was still safe.

"Okay, but if that's not why would you want advice from people who aren't even good enough to be on the Squad? It makes no sense," Megan said.

"Sorry I'm late." Lily burst in the door. Then she skidded to a stop. "What'd I miss?"

"You missed me telling everyone about Harper at lunch today," Riley said. "After she ditched us, I saw her."

"Oh, no," Lily said, and then before I realized what was happening, she continued, "They know about you and *The Little Mermaid*?" As soon as she said it, her eyes got wide and she clamped her hand over her mouth as she realized what she'd just done.

Oh. No.

"Wait, what?" Megan said.

"Nothing!" I said loudly, but everyone's attention was on Lily.

"*The Little Mermaid*?" Lily said. "Riley said she 'discovered'?"

"Riley discovered mermaids?!" Trina got really excited. "Real ones?"

"No, Trina," Megan said, rolling her eyes. "Riley didn't discover real mermaids."

"Oh. I'd love to meet a mermaid," Trina said, disappointed. "Oh wait, do you mean Harper's musical?"

"That's it! *The Little Mermaid* is our school musical!" Riley said.

"I thought you just said you knew that!" Lily said to her. She turned to me, upset. But I couldn't get mad at her. It wasn't her fault.

"You're in your school musical?" Megan asked.

"Yes—but I'm only in one dance," I said. "I didn't audition or anything. My English teacher asked me to help out."

"Wait, when you couldn't practice with me, is that where you were?" Megan said. "Hmm. Does Vanessa know about this?"

Er. Not yet.

"Megan," I said. I needed to deflect. I tried to appeal to her ego. "Speaking of *The Little Mermaid*, you look like a Disney princess!"

That was weak.

"Do you think?" she said. "Which one?"

It worked! I couldn't believe it worked. The rest of the girls, including Lily, who winked at me, began debating which princess she looked most like. And totally forgot about playing detective and figuring out where I really was at the last practice. My secret was safe. For now.

When we got out of the car, Hailey went right into the house and to her room without saying anything.

I'd better go stretch, I'd better go do my homework, I'd better . . .

Something about Hailey's face, though, got to me. I hadn't hung out with her in days. I realized something.

I knocked on her bedroom door.

"Hi." I peeked my head in. "What are you doing?"

"Nothing. Just watching videos," Hailey said, not looking up from her tablet.

"Are you watching *Hailey on the Daily*?" I sat down on the bed next to her.

"What? No," Hailey said. "I'm not even doing that anymore."

"You aren't?" I asked her. "Why not?"

"It was stupid," she said. "Everything I tried didn't work."

"You shouldn't quit. You're a good filmmaker!" I protested. "Even Megan was impressed with what you filmed of our dances. That was really helpful, by the way."

"She was just being nice," Hailey grumbled.

"I thought your show was funny," I said.

"It didn't work without you," Hailey complained. "I didn't have anyone to help me."

"I'm sorry," I said. "Once I'm done with this play and the solos—"

"Then you'll get the solo and you'll just have to rehearse all the time," Hailey said.

"No, I promise I'll help you," I said. "It's fun. I like your show."

"There's no show," Hailey muttered, and went back to watching her tablet.

I felt really bad. I went downstairs, where my mom was working on her laptop.

"Hi, honey," she said. "Hang on one second. Just working on a client's spreadsheet . . . and done. What's up?"

"Hailey seems sad," I said.

"Yeah, she's going through a little rough patch adjusting to the move, I think," Mom said. "I'm hoping she can make some good friends in school. I don't think it's clicking for her yet, but she'll get there."

I couldn't do anything about it—or could I? I spotted the video camera on the kitchen counter, and on my way out I grabbed it. I filled up my water bottle and went to my room. I grabbed one of my stretch bands and looped it around my feet to loosen myself up. I rewound the video camera and watched.

"Welcome to *Hailey on the Daily*!"

Hailey was adorable. I scrolled through and smiled when I saw our cake disaster. Then I saw some footage I'd never seen.

"Hi, it's *Hailey on the Daily*. Today, we're going to make slime!" I watched as Hailey tried to make slime, smiling until she accidentally knocked over the bowl and slime went everywhere. I bet my mom loved that.

But it was her next that episode threw me off.

"*Hailey on the Daily* is going to do . . . dance moves!" Hailey proclaimed. "I got to watch—and film—my sister's dance team rehearsal today. They're really good. I learned a move from it, though, and I'm going to share it with you on my show!"

Hailey tried to demonstrate one of our combinations. One, two, three, four . . . five, six, seven, eight. She did pretty well until she stumbled on a turn.

"I'm not good like my sister is," she said. "I only get to take one class. Ugh, I'm such a fail."

Then her face fell and the camera went dark. Hailey was so fun on camera, and you could tell she really liked it. Just because a few things in her videos didn't work out, didn't mean she was a fail! I felt even worse after watching that.

That gave me an idea. I jumped up and connected the video camera to my laptop. And I got to work.

An hour later, I knocked on Hailey's door.

"What?" she asked me.

"I want to show you something," I said. I sat down with my laptop and clicked on the video I'd just put together.

"Welcome to *Hailey on the Daily*!" Hailey said. Some cheesy music I'd found quickly played, and text came up: *Hailey on the Daily . . . Fail-y!*

"Wait." Hailey frowned. She pressed pause.

"No, it's fun, I promise," I said to her. "You were just saying how we—not you—screwed up some of those? So you can't have a show? I think the show's even better. You're hilarious. Just watch."

"Whatever." She scowled, but clicked play.

A montage of scenes came on, with Hailey and sometimes me. All of the funniest moments. Hailey started to smile, and then she started to laugh.

"My editing isn't that good," I said. "But look how funny your show is!"

"And that's it for *Hailey on the Daily*!" on-screen Hailey said. And I'd put text over it saying: *Fail-y!*

"Look what a good host you are!" I said. "You can't give up your show because you don't know how to make a cake yet. You know what my old dance teacher in Connecticut used to say to us: *'You're talented. But even if you weren't, you shouldn't give up! Work harder and learn from your mistakes! And follow your dreams!'"*

"Aw," Hailey said, looking embarrassed. "Thanks. But actually it got kind of boring. I'm looking for another talent. I think I found it."

Hailey held up her phone, where she had an app of a girl playing a cover of a song in her room.

"Singing star," Hailey said. "Here, I've been practicing." Hailey showed me.

"You are a pretty good singer," I agreed.

"I want to take lessons, though," Hailey said. "I think I

should before I go to the recording studio, you know?"

"Sure." I nodded, holding back a smile. Hey, she was a good singer. Maybe my little sister could make music videos! "Want me to talk to Mom about having you take some lessons? I can get a ride from Lily and make more time for you."

"Would you?" Hailey grinned. "That's cool. Also, they have a holiday chorus in school. I was thinking about doing that. Maybe. I don't know anyone."

"You should definitely sign up for that," I told her. "I didn't know anyone at DanceStarz. Or in the school musical."

"Okay," Hailey said. "I will."

"Speaking of dance and the musical, I promise I'll spend more time with you when they're less crazy."

"You just spent time with me." Hailey shrugged. "Now leave. I'm busy practicing my vocals."

I laughed, but then when she looked back down at her tablet, I realized she was serious. Hey, I was glad she was feeling happier. I was glad I could cheer her on.

Now I had to do the same for me.

After the stress of competition dance, the musical was becoming a happy place. Everyone was always so supportive and enthusiastic! And it was such an exciting time: tech week!

Tech week was when we rehearsed with all of the lights and sound and set and props. The final day of tech week would be dress rehearsal on Thursday, the day before the real show. It was going to be so exciting!

I walked into the auditorium smiling.

That didn't last long.

"I cannot even believe her!" one of the seaweeds said.

People were in clumps whispering. Flounder and Frankie were sitting on the side of the stage, and they waved me over.

"What's up?" I asked.

"Drammaa," Flounder sang out and shook his head. "So Aquata was already mad at Zora before—"

"Because Aquata really wanted the part of Ursula." Frankie nodded.

"Well, that's not Zora's fault—" I started to say, but they kept going.

"But anyway, I guess Aquata told people Zora can't sing the high notes," Flounder said. "And Zora told Aquata she found out and Aquata just ran off crying and says she's going to quit the play."

"Oh, no!" I said. "That's really sad. I thought everything here was so happy and perfect!"

They both burst into laughter.

"You missed last night," Frankie said. "Two of the seaweeds got in a fight because they both like the same guy. . . ."

I sat up straight. *Uh-oh*.

"King Triton," Zora specified. *Whew*. I was sure other people would have crushes on Drew, but I didn't want to even think about a fight about that.

Ariel came over and sat down next me.

"It's gets really stressful when the show gets closer." She sighed. "Is it like that at dance?"

"Ha! It's like that nonstop. It's like we always have a show coming up," I said. "But wait, it's not like it's all bad. We also get super close bonding!"

"We could use some of that bonding now," Ariel said. "You missed a lot of tension the past twenty-four hours."

Weirdly, I felt like that was a bad thing. I missed a lot of stuff by only being a substitute dancer in one scene. I knew that going through the whole process together often meant you got closer with everyone, through good times and bad. I felt left out.

Just then, Aquata came back in through the backstage door, with red eyes. Zora followed her, and I could see her eyes were also red. And behind them both, Mrs. Elliott.

"Let's get back to work!" Mrs. Elliott clapped her hands. "Oyster and pearl dancers on deck!"

"She's staying!" everyone was whispering. "She's staying!"

Whew! I thought. I looked over at Zora and tried to give her an encouraging face, but she was looking down. I tried the same with Aquata, but she was whispering with some of her mer-sisters.

It was time for me to refocus on dance. I ran off to the left wing to wait for my entrance with the other under-the-sea creatures. I closed my eyes to get into the headspace to perform, but couldn't ignore the whispering around me.

"Did they make up?"

"Who started it?"

"Aquata is such a drama queen," Frankie said snarkily. "If she left, I was going to suggest Harper take her role."

"Uh, NO!" I gasped. "No, no!"

I hadn't even thought of that, that people would think I could substitute for her. I should have felt flattered, but the thought of attempting to take on anything else right now made me want to throw up.

"Harper wanted to take Aquata's role?"

Oh, no! One of the seaweeds thought that! I did NOT want that to become a rumor! Ugh, now I really wanted to throw up.

"NO!" I said loudly, looking right at her. "Nobody should quit! I just want to dance my dance!"

I climbed into my oyster shell and fumed. Ugh! I just wanted being in the musical to go back to being all happy times. Why was there drama in drama, too? I guessed I shouldn't have been surprised. If dancing onstage was stressful and competitive, why wouldn't being in a huge play?

Sebastian started singing, and I waited to be rolled out onstage.

"No, no!" I could hear Mrs. Elliott calling out. "Try that again."

After a moment to reset, Sebastian started the song again. I could hear some of the sea creatures run out to dance. Under the sea! Inside my seashell! *La la la*, I sang quietly to myself.

It was a little bit cramped in the oyster shell. Could we get on with this? I lay on my back and pushed my legs against the shell. I squirmed around to get comfortable, which I did by lying down with my feet up.

"Courtney and Frankie! Two beats earlier!" Mrs. Elliott yelled. "Take it from the top."

Sebastian started singing again.

It was actually kind of warm and cozy in my seashell. Like a little nest from the outside world. I closed my eyes and breathed deeply. Maybe I could just stay in my little shell and shut out the drama drama . . . Ah.

I was floating in the water, dancing. Oh, in a beautiful mermaid outfit. Oh, nice! I'd turned into a mermaid. I twirled in the water, admiring my long, beautiful tail. Wait, was I dancing with someone? Yes, yes, I was! Was it . . . Drew? I squinted in the dark, murky water to see, and then the lights underwater suddenly turned on and it wasn't Eric! It was Megan, dressed as Ursula! And she yelled at me. "Give me your voice, Harper!" And then she had a trident and shot a lightning bolt at me!

"NOOO!" I screamed.

I blinked my eyes open to find a bright streaming spotlight on me. Apparently, I'd fallen asleep and meanwhile, the shell had been wheeled out on the stage and fallen open for my big reveal, when I was supposed to pop up and lift my leg into a standing leg hold to oohs and aahs. Instead, I was curled into a little ball, blinking like a deer in headlights. And screaming about an eel. I was totally discombobulated. And I set off a chain reaction.

Sebastian's singing faltered as he got confused. Some of the sea creatures jumped up on cue, but others stayed crouched down waiting for me. Some people were dancing, while others were still waiting for me, causing people to bump into one another—and me.

I jumped out of the shell too early and bumped into Flounder, who tripped—right into the bubble-making machine. He must have hit some switch, and a massive amount of bubbles started to churn out of it at an alarming speed.

We were surrounded by bubbles.

"I can't see!" someone yelled. Bubbles were everywhere! Popping! And when they popped, the bubble liquid got all over the stage. The slippery, soapy bubble liquid.

ACK!

Now everyone was slipping and sliding into one another, all over the stage.

Bam! Bam! Bam! A few people fell down, and then couldn't get their footing because of the liquid bubbles.

"CUT!" Mrs. Elliott yelled. "Cut, cut, cut! NOBODY MOVE!"

Everyone froze as the bubbles cleared from the stage. Which was a mixed blessing, because I could see everyone staring at me.

"Sorry, sorry, sorry!" I apologized profusely to everyone. "Sorry!"

Then I heard Aquata whisper: "She only has one dance and she messes it up?"

My face was already flaming red, but then I saw Drew looking my way sympathetically. Ugh, ugh, ugh. I think my face basically spontaneously combusted in flames.

"Walk or crawl carefully stage left!" Mrs. Elliott told us.

I crawled offstage in shame, my hands sticky from bubble juice.

"Well, apparently that's an early wrap for today." Mrs. Elliott let out a huge sigh of disappointment. And I knew it was mostly at me.

"Stage manager, call the custodian. We have to clean up this mess."

I was definitely relieved to get out of there.

*A*fter that disaster of a rehearsal, I headed up to my room to try and calm down. I was in there for a while when there was a knock on my bedroom door.

I didn't answer, so whoever it was would go away. I was curled up in my purple round floofy chair, with a blanket over my head and Mo on my lap.

I had a ton of homework to do, but I couldn't concentrate because I kept thinking of how embarrassing it was when I was doing my one dance. Like Aquata said, I had only one dance to do. And I hadn't even gotten past the first move.

Bleh.

I thought about everyone staring at me, from the sea

creatures to Mrs. Elliott and, of course, Drew. Ugh, ugh, ugh. I petted Mo almost frantically, trying to erase the memory of falling asleep in the cozy shell. . . .

I realized that the way I was curled up in my round chair was actually a lot like how I'd been curled up in the round shell and—ugh!

There was another knock.

"I'm sleeping!" I called out.

"You're obviously not sleeping, since you just answered me!" Hailey replied. "Say *come in.*"

"Go away," I mumbled.

I heard the door open.

"I said go away," I said, under my blanket.

"Oh, I thought you said *come in!*" Hailey said, cheerfully and untruthfully. "Wait, where are you?"

Mo betrayed me by barking from under the covers. I felt the covers ripped off me, and Hailey was standing over me.

"What?" I said.

"I heard about what happened," Hailey said. "I wanted to help."

"You heard? How did you hear?"

"Quinn," Hailey said. Quinn? How did Riley's sister hear I embarrassed myself in school musical rehearsal? That made no sense. "She heard Riley talking to Megan about it. Poor Lily."

"Wait. Poor Lily?" I was confused.

"Yeah, I guess she ran off crying," Hailey said.

"So this isn't about me falling asleep onstage in the musical?" I asked.

"You fell asleep onstage? Ha! That's hilarious!" Hailey replied. "No, I'm talking about what Megan and Riley said to Lily at dance. Megan asked Lily if she was going to show up at solos, and when Lily said yes, Riley said she shouldn't because she'd be embarrassed."

"Why would she be embarrassed?" I asked.

"Megan told Lily she's only good at ballet and the reason Vanessa gave her a tumbling routine was to make sure Lily didn't have a chance at the solo. Everyone is going to feel sorry for her. Didn't you hear her say it?"

"No," I said, furious that Megan would even say that. "I had to miss rehearsal today to do the play. Thanks for telling me, Hailey. I've got to text Lily."

"Okay," Hailey said, pausing. "Tell her when I filmed her I thought she was a good dancer!"

"I will," I told her. I threw the covers off. Mo jumped up. *Oops, sorry, Mo.* I grabbed my phone and texted Lily.

????

I saw that she read it. The little bubble went on and off, like she was thinking of how to answer. Nothing came up. I texted again.

Are you at Sugar Plums?

This time she answered.

No. Home.

I knew what I had to do. Lily had been so supportive of me since day one. She knew how hard I danced and that I'd been doing competitions way longer than she had. But it had to be annoying to hear people talking about Megan and me having the best opportunities. And to hear me complaining how busy I was—being a little bit of the star. And now this?

I needed to be there for her.

I ran downstairs to ask my mom if she could drive me over to Lily's. Surprisingly, she understood and said yes, and even more surprisingly, Hailey didn't complain when we had to go.

When I rang Lily's doorbell, I texted her, It's me.

Her father answered the door.

"Harper, how nice to see you!" he said. "We've missed you. Lily's out at the pool, so just go on back."

I went around the side of the house to the pool. Lily was

out there. She was lying on a pool floatie with sunglasses on—
and waterproof headphones.

"Lily!" I called out, but she didn't hear me. I tried to splash
water at her but couldn't reach to get her attention. I went over
and picked up a mini beach ball from the side of the pool and
tossed it gently at her.

Oops! It hit her right in the face and knocked her sunglasses off.

"AHH!" Lily sat up abruptly, flipping the float over. When she
resurfaced, sputtering, she saw me. "What the heck, Harper?"

"Sorry, sorry!" I said. "I couldn't get your attention!"

"Wait, what are doing here?" she asked.

"Um," I said. "I had some free time! I just wanted to hang
out!"

"You heard," Lily said. "Great. Is that the big gossip at
DanceStarz? I'm humiliated!"

She flopped back and sank underwater. I waited. Lily actually could hold her breath a long time. I decided not to wait. I
took a running start—and I jumped into the pool.

In my clothes.

I swam under until I was right in front of Lily. It was a
little challenging because my tank top kept floating up and

threatening to strangle me, but I made it to her. She had plugged her nose, but her eyes were open and wide, looking at me. She popped up to the surface, and I followed her.

"What are you doing?" she half laughed. "You're in your clothes!"

"I know," I said. "I just wanted to make you laugh."

Lily flopped on her back into a float. I joined her. We drifted for a minute, looking at the clouds in the sky.

"You're always cheering me up," I said. "Especially when I have my . . . awkward moments. So I wanted to finally return the favor."

"Your moments are different," Lily said.

"By 'different' do you mean worse?" I asked.

"No, I mean, okay, you might trip over something, but—"

"In front of an entire parade!" I interjected.

"Okay, that was pretty bad," Lily had to admit.

"That's way more humiliating than something the Bunheads said," I said. "They're always saying mean things. Well, two of them."

"But you always bounce back and then get picked for things. You're so good at dancing that it makes up for it. Mine hurts because it's true."

"It's not true," I said.

"Vanessa never thought I had any shot at the solo," Lily said. "The only thing I can dance is ballet. And now I'm going to get up there and humiliate myself in front of the whole studio with a dumb tumbling routine."

"Your routine isn't dumb," I said. "I thought Vanessa gave it to you because you said you were tired of ballet. And you're so bouncy and fun."

"Well, everyone else at DanceStarz will believe what Megan said," Lily said.

"Well, you'll just have to show them differently at our next competition," I said.

Lily laughed.

"What?" I asked.

"You make that sound so easy," she said. "I'm just not as good a dancer as you are."

"We'll practice together," I said. "I'm almost done with the musical—OH! THE MUSICAL! AUUUGH! I didn't even tell you what happened to me!"

I told Lily the story of falling asleep in the shell and waking up disoriented.

Lily tried to keep a straight face. But when I got to the part about the bubble machine, she let out a snort.

"Sorry." She snorted again. Then she cracked up. "We are so embarrassing."

"I knowwww," I groaned. "I had to literally crawl off the stage in shame."

"Well, it's nice we can be embarrassing together," Lily said.

Lily was seriously such a good friend. There was something else I thought about telling her.

"Okay, you want to know the other worst part about it?" I asked her. "I did it in front of . . . there's this . . . Drew . . ."

"Oh, that guy you sat across from at the lunch table?" she said. "Drew? He's in my math class. I knew it! I saw you smiling at him!"

"Ughhhh, was I that obvious?" I groaned again.

"Just to me," Lily said. "I don't think anyone else noticed. Well, maybe him. But he was smiling back at you!"

He was? I grinned for a minute, until I remembered I'd humiliated myself in front of him.

"It could have been worse," I admitted. "He had been in my dream for a second. What if I'd yelled, *Drew*?"

We both cracked up.

"Instead it turned into a nightmare," Lily said. "Why is Megan haunting both of us?"

"Yeah, we need to stop that," I said. "We need to stop letting

Megan get to us! In fact, let's one of us get this solo dance!"

My mom came into the backyard, through the door.

"Uh . . . Harper?" My mom interrupted our moment. "Are you swimming in your clothes?"

Oops.

"I—"

"I don't even want to know." Mom sighed. "Lily, we can drive you as well if you'd like."

"Thanks," Lily said. "I'll text my mom so she knows not to leave Sugar Plums to pick me up. Then I'll change really quick!"

"Me too!" I said. Fortunately, I had my dance bag ready to go in the car. I went to get it, and when I came back, Lily was in her leotard and shorts and on her phone. When she saw me, she looked up—and looked upset.

"I don't want to make this day worse, but"—she paused—"I think we're too late."

She held up her phone and I took a look with her.

Megan had just posted a story from DanceStarz's back office. She was filming her mother looking inside a box.

"It was worth it!" her mother was saying. "It's stunning! Look at all the sequins!"

The camera turned off, but not before I saw a peek of what

was in the box. A flash of white material sparkled in the camera light, before the story cut off.

"Was that . . . ?" I looked at Lily, and she nodded.

"I think it's her costume," Lily said. "And that means . . ."

Megan got the solo.

19

*Y*ou two are awfully quiet," Mom said as she drove us to DanceStarz.

"They're sad," Hailey said from the backseat.

Lily and I looked at each other. We hadn't realized we'd been that obvious.

"Ah," Mom said. Fortunately, she didn't push any further.

I mean, it wasn't like I hadn't expected it. Megan was known as the premier dancer at DanceStarz. She definitely had been there longer than me. I'd figured she'd get the solo. I just thought I'd have more of a chance to prove myself first. I didn't realize Vanessa was so close to picking the solo already. That it wouldn't be sprung on us, like Megan smiling at us from the phone.

"Don't be sad," Hailey said.

"It'll be fine." I sighed.

"It's just we didn't get picked for something at dance," Lily told her.

"Pffft!" Hailey said. "Make a *Hailey on the Daily* Fail-y!"

Lily looked at me, confused.

"Didn't you say not to give up?" Hailey said. "Just like you told me before: follow your dreams!"

I leaned back against the headrest.

"She's not wrong," Lily said.

"It is true," I admitted. "I guess maybe we can take my own advice."

"If you want, I can film you two dancing and failing," Hailey offered. "Do you want me to come to your rehearsal again and film everything you do wrong?"

"Okay, that might be a little much," I said, starting to laugh.

"I have to agree," Lily said.

"But seriously, Hailey, you're right," I told her. "I'm not going to give up just because this one thing didn't go my way."

"Even when Vanessa announces that Megan is the soloist," Lily said.

"We should be supportive of her," I agreed.

"Wow, Hailey, you're so wise," Lily said.

"Thank you," Hailey said solemnly. "It's true."

My mom's mouth twitched as she held back a smile. I had to admit, Hailey had taken a huge weight off my shoulders. I decided I really would do my best to go into DanceStarz with a positive attitude.

So when I walked into the Studio B, I smiled at the Bun-heads.

"Congratulations," I said to Megan.

"Ooh, what did you do?!" Trina clapped her hands.

"I saw the story," I told her. "With your dress."

Megan's eyes opened wide.

"Uh, what dress?" she asked. She looked both startled and a little nervous at the same time.

"Your dress for the solo?" I asked.

The door opened and Vanessa walked in.

Megan shot me another weird look. Before I could say anything, Vanessa clapped her hands to get our attention.

"Good afternoon, Squad!" Vanessa said. "Please join me in a circle. I have an important announcement."

Here we go. We all went and sat in a circle on the floor around Vanessa. Here was when Vanessa would announce that Megan got the solo dance. The very first solo dance for the most competitive dance team DanceStarz has ever had. It would be a shining moment for both Megan and for DanceStarz—

Vanessa interrupted my imaginary speech with the real version.

"You all know that we are about to reach a milestone at DanceStarz. One of you will perform the first solo dance at the highest competition level we have ever had. So, with great excitement, I present . . ."

We all nodded. I plastered a smile on my face to be ready for the announcement that it was Megan.

The door opened.

"Your solo costumes!"

One of Vanessa's assistants wheeled in a rack with garment bags hanging on them. Nobody moved. No one said anything.

HUH?

"Should I try that again?" Vanessa looked confused. "I present, your costumes!"

She raised her arm with a flourish and pointed to the rack.

"This is not the reception I was expecting," Vanessa said. "You may go get your costumes."

"Um," Lily spoke hesitantly. "*Costumes?* Plural?"

"Why, yes," Vanessa said. She looked at us, perplexed. "I thought you'd all be a little more excited to see them."

"We all get our costumes?" Riley asked.

"Well, yes." Vanessa looked confused. "Why wouldn't you?"

We all looked at Megan. She looked away.

"We thought only the soloist would actually get her costume," I answered. "Like, as a reward."

"You thought I'd have you choose costumes but not get to wear them?" Vanessa asked. "No, no. You know that's not how I would work or 'reward' you—the reward is the solo itself. Even if you don't perform the solo for the competition, you'll each still have the opportunity to perform in other places. Maybe other competitions, maybe more parades. I want all of you to be ready to go at any time."

"All of us?" Lily piped up.

"All of you," Vanessa said firmly.

"Are you announcing who got the solo today?" Riley spoke up.

"No," Vanessa said. "I don't have enough information yet to make that decision."

She didn't? She hadn't picked Megan? She hadn't decided? I figured it was the case since we all had our costumes, but still.

I still had a chance?! YES!

"Now, what are you waiting for? Don't you want to try on your costumes?" Vanessa said.

That got us going.

"YES!" We all jumped up and ran over to our costumes.

Mine was even more gorgeous than it had been in the catalog. The orchid color was a light lavender with a little bit of shine. I ran into the dressing room with everyone, and we pulled on our costumes. I ran back into the dance studio and looked in the mirror before anyone else had gotten there.

The mesh looked really nice against my now-tanned-from-Florida skin. I twirled my hips so the skirt could float around me. I loved it. I picked at my sleeves a bit. They were too long, but fortunately nothing that my mom couldn't shorten.

Lily came running in with hers on. The coppery color of her crop top and shorts reflected in the light, so she was literally shining.

"You look awesome!" I told her.

"Thanks!" she said. She did a roundoff back handspring in excitement.

Trina and Riley came back into the studio. Trina struck a pose in her hot pink–and–black tap outfit, looking sharp. Riley shimmered in her multicolored costume, making it sparkle like a strobe light.

"You guys look great!" Lily and I told them.

"Where's Megan?" Lily asked.

185

"It's taking her a minute. Hers is really complicated," Riley said. She checked her phone. "Oh, she needs some help. Be right back."

"Harper," Trina said once Riley had left. "How is your *Mermaid* cast doing with their dancing? My sister and I were just talking about how fun that was. Everyone was so nice."

"Aw," I said. "They're mostly good. Actually, the last rehearsal I was the one who messed up the dance."

"She ran into a giant fish and knocked over the bubble machine," Lily said solemnly.

"Oh, I love bubbles!" Trina clapped her hands happily. "That sounds fun! Maybe not the giant fish, though. That could be creepy. Possibly smelly, if it was out of the water."

"Not a real one!" I tried to hold back a laugh. "Flounder. He was in costume. Remember Flounder from when you rehearsed with us?"

"Oh, he was the cute one, right?" Trina said. "He actually follows me now and likes my stories."

I hadn't actually thought of him as "the cute one," but . . . that was sweet! I was happy my friends could get along from both worlds.

The door swung open, and Riley made an announcement: "Presenting . . . Megan! In her solo costume!" Inwardly, I rolled my eyes that Megan would make such an entrance.

But when she walked in, I actually understood why.

"Oh my gosh!" Trina and I both gasped in unison. Lily's eyes went wide.

Megan's dress was unbelievable. It looked like something out of a royal wedding. You could barely see the white silk underneath all of the glittering crystals.

"That's crazy beautiful," I said.

"I know, right?" Megan preened. She walked slowly into the room and around in a circle so we could see the full view. "My mom paid extra and had them add four hundred sequins to the top."

"Whoa." I shook my head. That was extravagant, but I had to admit it looked amazing.

"That's probably why her mom got to see the costume first," Lily whispered to me. I nodded. Vanessa came in to the room and admired our outfits.

"You all look fabulous," she said. "You're all going to represent DanceStarz very well in those costumes."

We thanked her.

"Lily, Trina," she said. "Looks like those fit perfectly. You may take them off. Trina, looks like you have a little issue with the jacket fit? And Harper, you'll need to take up your sleeves.

If your parents need a tailor, I can recommend one. Megan, that looks like it works. . . ."

"Yup. Yup, it does. Can I take it off now?" Megan said. "I don't want to get it icky."

"Yes, you all may," Vanessa said. "When you get back, we'll do drills. Hard-core today. The clock is ticking for competition."

We all groaned about drills. But we cheered ourselves up by taking selfies and pictures with one another in our costumes before we took them off.

When I went back into the dressing room, I decided to live up to my promise to Lily. I went to stand next to Megan.

"Why did you say that Vanessa told you that only one of us would get an outfit?"

"Well, I never actually said that, but I honestly thought that's what would happen," Megan said. "And when my mom was talking to her about the sequins for my costume . . ."

Her voice trailed off. That's when I noticed her eyes were slightly red and puffy. It looked like she'd been crying.

"Oh, you thought you already had the solo?" I said quietly.

Megan didn't say anything, but she didn't have to. I knew that meant that she did. Maybe she'd thought Vanessa was announcing that today and had been just as shocked today as

I'd been. But she would have been disappointed. Aw. I reached out and touched her arm sympathetically.

"Don't touch my costume," Megan snapped. "Do you know how much four hundred extra sequins costs?"

Oookay. I pulled my hand back. My moment of sympathy was gone pretty quickly.

"I need it in pristine condition," Megan said. She paused and then looked right into my eyes. "For my solo. And by 'my solo,' I mean . . . MY solo."

She flipped her hair and turned the other way. I'd been dismissed.

We all went back into the studio. Vanessa stood in front of the room.

"How do you like your costumes?" she asked, and we all cheered. "I was hoping this would be one more motivator. I've decided the time has arrived to choose the soloist."

We all froze.

"Not today," Vanessa said. "I've spent time with each of you and your dances, and you're all performing very well. But really what it comes down to is how you perform onstage. Under pressure, alone, in front of people who are judging you. Each of you will perform your solo in front of an audience—here at Dance-Starz."

She took out some papers from her bag and handed one to each of us. They were flyers.

**Come see the Squad perform
their new solo dances!
STUDIO A
Sunday at seven p.m.**

Oh, that was both exciting and overwhelming! We'd get to show off our dances to everyone at the studio. But how we did would determine our chance to do the solo! I had to get ready and—

That's when it hit me. I raised my hand.

"Sunday?" I asked. "This Sunday?"

"Yes," Vanessa said. "During your regular Squad rehearsal time."

I had my musical on Sunday. I calculated in my head. The musical was at three, and then I'd been planning to skip DanceStarz that night. I could pull it off. But it would be close. And I needed to tell Vanessa about the musical. It was time. This was going to be really difficult. I just hoped Vanessa wouldn't get mad at me. I wouldn't blame her. I was mad at myself for not telling her earlier.

"I was going to tell you," I said. "I just didn't want you to question my commitment, especially with the solos coming up."

"Okay . . ."

"I wasn't planning on doing it, but my teacher asked me. I didn't audition or anything, and it fell into my lap, honest," I said.

"Harper," Vanessa started. But now that I had begun talking, I couldn't stop.

"It's only one dance!" I said. "I learned the choreo really fast! And rehearsals were mostly during lunch! Except the one time Megan wanted us to do the partner routine so I'd get it."

Vanessa gave me a look. "Harper, I have no idea what you're talking about. Slow down and explain to me what is going on."

"Oh," I said. "Sorry, I'm so nervous. I'm in my school musical."

"Congratulations!" Vanessa said.

Oh.

"Thanks?" I said. "The thing is, I don't want this to interfere with dancing. I'm one hundred percent committed to the competition."

"I'm happy to hear that," Vanessa said.

"Does this"—I hesitated—"does this affect my chance to be in the competition?"

She knew I meant a solo.

"I'll be honest and tell you I don't know," Vanessa said, and I slumped down. "There are many factors. Dedication is one of them. I don't want you to spread yourself too thin. But being part of your school doesn't mean you aren't dedicated."

That sounded a little more promising.

"It's actually helping with my dancing," I said tentatively. "I asked the actors to help me express emotions, like you wanted."

"Sounds like you're making the most of it," Vanessa said. "My brother played football, but he also took a ballet class with me because the dance skills helped him as an athlete. When is the musical?"

"This weekend," I said.

"This weekend?" Vanessa said.

"I know, it's bad timing," I said. "But the shows are just Friday and Saturday . . . and Sunday is a matinee. It will be over with before the solo competition!"

"Well, it sounds like you're very busy," Vanessa said, "but working hard. Are you sure you're going to be up for it? That's a lot."

"YES!" I practically shouted at her. "Uh, sorry! I'm just . . . Yes! I will be."

Saturday night, the musical. Sunday afternoon, the musical—

And Sunday night, solo auditions.

ACK! That was a lot.

Would I really be up for that?

was so excited about my solo dance costume that when I got to dress rehearsal for *The Little Mermaid*, I almost forgot that I'd be getting another dress! I waited for the costume person to call my name for my turn.

"Ta-da!" Zora came out in her costume, which was super dramatic as she swished her tentacles around.

"You look amazing!" I said, and Zora curtsied. We were in the dressing room behind the middle school stage. Suddenly, it really felt like I was under the sea: Zora's sea witch costume, the fish with their puffy felt costumes trying not to bump into each other. Seaweed, with tall reedy hats, waving around.

"I can't believe it's already dress rehearsal!" Courtney said. "I'm freaking out!"

"Where's our Pearl?" the costume person called my name. I went into see mine. Because I'd been cast late, I hadn't had any fittings yet, so it was the first time even seeing my costume.

Ohhh. The costume person carried out an ivory-colored dress with a fitted tank top covered in pearls, and then a satin flowy skirt and held it up for me. It was so pretty. I would wear cream-colored ballet slippers with it.

I pulled the costume on. I loved how it looked! It actually reminded me a little of Megan's solo dress—a less elaborate version. I walked out onstage, feeling a little bit shy in my fancy dress surrounded by giant fish and crabs and seaweed costumes and humans.

And, of course, my eye went right to Drew. His costume looked really simple but good on him. Jeans, a white shirt, and a red belt. Right when I looked up at him, he looked back at me. And he smiled. He was smiling at me!

Hee!

I gave him a thumbs-up.

A thumbs-up? What was I doing?! I quickly put my hand behind my back. Then I gave him a weird smile. But he still smiled back. Then everyone turned their attention behind me.

Ariel had walked out in her mermaid costume.

"WOW," people gasped.

Ariel looked like the ultimate Little Mermaid, with a long red wig, a royal blue tank top, and—of course—her mermaid tail.

"You look awesome," I told her as she walked by.

"Thanks. I think I need practice walking, though," she said, laughing as she shuffled past me.

And dress rehearsals began.

Dress rehearsals are notorious for being the time when things tend to fall apart. And we were no exception. People forgot lines, people forgot dances, people even forgot people during some of the partner routines. But unlike last rehearsal, Mrs. Elliott didn't seem to be stressed out. Defective bubble machines were not normal, but all of this preshow stuff seemed to be.

"Bad dress rehearsal means good opening night!" Mrs. Elliott called out cheerfully after someone stumbled a little onstage.

My own dress rehearsal at least went better than the whole falling-asleep-in-the-oyster-shell incident. I missed a step or two, but otherwise, it was fine.

But I was more worried about what comes after dress rehearsal.

THE REAL SHOW.

21

*S*howtime! I'm onstage, inside the shell, getting ready to start my number! I can hear the music for "Under the Sea" playing, and I jump out of the shell and started dancing. But "Under the Sea" stops playing . . . and my solo music for DanceStarz starts instead! I start to automatically do my own solo routine, but that means I run right into Flounder.

Uh-oh.

As I scramble back to try and get back into place, I accidentally run into Drew and knock him right off the stage into the pit! But instead of musicians being in the pit, he lands on a row of dance competition judges, who jump up and start to boo!

Their scorecards all read big, fat, O.

"Harper!" Vanessa yells. "What happened out there?"

"Everything was getting mixed up!" I cry.

Then I see Mrs. Elliott stomp over.

"Harper!"

"Harper!"

"Harper?"

Oh no, not again. I opened my eyes hesitantly, and realized I had fallen asleep AGAIN in English class.

"Sorry, sorry," I said to Mrs. Elliott, who was standing in front of the class. Naturally, Riley was cracking up at me. I flushed beet red, hoping I wouldn't get into trouble.

"No worries," Mrs. Elliott replied. "I was just taking attendance. I know you're deep in thought to prepare for the school musical, which opens tonight. Let's use Harper as an example of intensity for writing today. As Harper shows us, when you're deep in thought you can tune out the outside world. This is a skill that we can actually learn while writing so you don't get distracted."

And she winked at me!

Riley and Naima stopped cracking up, and Riley scowled.

Ha! Take that! Also, I needed to thank Mrs. Elliott for saving me.

The rest of the school day went by in a blur. At lunch I sat with the cast, and everyone was unusually silent, except for occasional outbursts of "I'm so nervous!" and "I'm going to throw up!"

I only had the one dance and I was nervous! I couldn't imagine having so many lines and being one of the stars.

That night, the dressing room was crazy! Everyone was getting their costumes and makeup on. One of the high school helpers offered to help me helped me put on stage makeup, but I was used to doing it myself for competition dance. Foundation, face powder, and extra dark makeup so the stage lights didn't wash me out. I wound my hair up into a bun like Mrs. Elliott had asked me.

When I was done, I looked in the mirror. I was ready before pretty much everyone! I was so used to getting ready quickly in the craziness of having one or more dances in a day.

Everyone else was still racing around in a frenzy of bobby pins, hair spray, and mic packs.

"Harper, your makeup looks great," Mrs. Elliott commented. "Who helped you with that?"

"Oh, I did it myself," I told her. "I learned from dance."

"We're running behind," she said. "Would you mind helping the humans? They have pretty basic stage makeup."

"Okay!" I said. "Sure!"

"HUMANS!" Mrs. Elliott yelled. "Anyone who still needs makeup help?"

"I DO!" someone called out.

Drew! As if I weren't nervous enough! He was sitting in one of the folding chairs in his costume among the other humans.

"Uh." I went over to him and stood there. "Hi!"

"Hi!" he said. "Hey! Hi! You look great."

Oh! Ha! I could feel myself blushing from the compliment. We both stood there for a second before I realized he didn't know why I was there.

"I'm, um, supposed to help with makeup?" I said.

"Oh!" he said. "You? Uh. Okay."

"I mean, I don't have to," I backtracked. "I know how to do stage makeup for dance, so I told Mrs. Elliott I could help."

"No, no, it's cool," he said. "Well, it's a little weird. I don't usually get makeup on. We don't use it for baseball."

I took his stage makeup kit from him and dabbed some of the pancake onto the sponge.

"You play baseball?" I asked him. "Also, close your eyes so I don't blind you."

"Yeah, shortstop," he said, closing his eyes. "But when Mrs. Elliott asked me to do this play, I thought it could be fun. Plus, my parents thought it would look good if I did more outside of sports. And it's something different, I guess. Everything always seems the same around here, you know?"

I took out the eyebrow pencil and began to darken his brows so people in the way back of the auditorium could see his expressions from the stage.

"I kind of don't know." I laughed. "Everything has changed for me. New state, new school, new dance studio, now even this."

"You're right," said Drew. "Sorry, I was just thinking of me. I've lived here forever. Well, isn't it kind of cool you get to have a fresh start? You can do whatever you want."

"That's kind of true." I nodded. "I still feel kind of the same, though. Except I used to know my place."

"Seems like you're finding your place," Drew said. "Everyone here likes you. You should try out for the spring play."

"Maybe," I said, pleased. "I like it. But dance takes up pretty much my whole life, so adding anything like this to it is hard. You're doing good for your first play."

I got out the powder and started putting it on his face.

"I guess we'll find out tonight," he said. "I'll probably screw up the dance steps and forget my lines and—*Cough! Cough! Cough!*"

He spat out some powder, which I may have intentionally powdered into his mouth.

"Did you do that on purpose?" He coughed.

"Maybe," I said. "Before our dance competitions, we're not allowed to be negative. Stay positive. You got this."

I snapped the makeup case shut.

"We all got this."

"You're not even a little nervous?" he asked me.

"Oh, I'm really nervous." I laughed. "I was acting."

"Told you that you should try out for the next play," he said.

He smiled at me. I smiled at him. We both smiled at each other.

Eee!

"Cast!" Mrs. Elliott broke the moment. "It's almost showtime! Places for Act One . . . Places, everybody!"

Drew jumped up.

"Break a leg!" we said to each other.

"Break a leg!" everyone yelled to one another. "Break a leg!"

It was time to get focused. It was showtime!

22

"Under the sea! Under the sea!"

I could hear Sebastian from inside the oyster shell, which was slightly vibrating from the loudspeakers around the stage. I knew that Ariel and Flounder would be standing near stage left, with all of the undersea characters dancing onto the stage.

And then my oyster shell began to move as they pushed me across the stage. It was almost time! Almost my time! I'd dance my first turn sequence.

No! No! Wrong dance!

Get it together, Harper, I thought to myself. I knew my cue was coming up and tried to focus again.

The shell opened. The lights dimmed and I stood up into my pose onstage and took a deep breath and—I could see my mom! My dad! Hailey! And my brother was here from college! That was a total surprise!

And wait! Was that . . .

Vanessa?

And Lily? Trina? Riley? And Megan? What were they doing here? Was I seeing things? Then the spotlight swung toward me, pretty much blinding me from seeing the audience anymore. Which was for the best, because I needed to get my head in the game.

It was time to dance!

I did my leg hold and then jumped off the shell. I wove among the sea creatures and Ariel and Sebastian. Sebastian did his salsa move with his crab hands in the air. The mer-sisters twirled me around. Flounder held his nose and did the swim. Then I did a quick waltz with Sebastian.

Under the sea! Darling, it's better—It *was* better! It was great.

I smiled at every one of the cast members as I passed them. My nerves were gone. This was what I loved to do: dance with people, whether with DanceStarz or in a big musical like this.

I was having a ton of fun. And I finally understood what

Vanessa was talking about. I finally got what my *Mermaid* cast was trying to tell me. About emotion. About feeling. And I was feeling GREAT!

Finally, my big moment came. I went center stage, took my prep, and did my turn series: five pirouettes and a high kick.

I ended in my split.

The audience erupted. Cheers! Clapping! I even heard Hailey yell, "Woo, Harper!"

Okay, having a solo was pretty cool too. Yeah, this was awesome. I soaked up my moment in the spotlight. Then I ran back to the oyster and jumped back in, and the sea creatures closed it up over me.

Once I was in the shell, I took a huge breath and let it out. *I did it! We did it! Yay!*

The curtain closed. I jumped out of the shell, and quickly high-fived everyone. I was on an adrenaline high from performing. We didn't make any mistakes, and I'd gotten amazing cheers for my solo dance! Then everyone else all ran off to get ready for their next scenes. It was a huge relief that it was over for me. Everyone else was onstage in a big group number, so I had time to myself. I made my way backstage to the little greenroom they had for us, where we had gotten ready earlier.

Whew! I had to process what just happened.

My brother was in the audience! My dance squad was in the audience! Vanessa was in the audience! I hoped I'd remembered to point my toes! I couldn't believe they'd all come to see me. It was such a surprise.

When cast members ran offstage and into the greenroom, where I was, we all hugged and high-fived each other.

"Harper, you were so good!" they told me. I told everyone they were great too.

And they were! When the show was over, we all got ready to go back onstage for the curtain call. I went up with the ensemble, holding hands with two of the seaweeds. But I got to take a quick step forward and get my own whistles and cheers. *Yay!*

When the curtain went down, Mrs. Elliott told us we'd done a great job. We all went out into the auditorium to see our family and friends. I wove through the crowd until I spotted my brother.

He was holding a bouquet of purple flowers for me!

"Good job, kid!" He gave me a hug. "You killed it!"

"Thanks!" I said. "Thanks for the flowers! How long are you home?"

"Just for tonight," he said. "So I'll see you back at the house. I'm so proud of you."

"Group hug!" Hailey ran up to us, dragging my parents by their hands.

"Harper, you were shining up there," my dad said. My mom just looked at me and sniffled back tears. She always got emotional when I danced.

"Did you see who was here?" she asked, looking around.

"The Squad and Vanessa?" I nodded. "Are they still here?"

"I'm not sure," Mom said.

"I'm going to look," I said. I hopped on the stage steps until I could see over everyone's heads. Then I spotted them at the side of the room. I jumped down and ran up to them. At first they didn't see me.

"Wow, hi!" I said. "Thanks for coming! I wasn't expecting that."

Lily gave me a huge smile and glanced at Vanessa, obviously waiting for her to speak first.

"Of course! We all wanted to support you," Vanessa said. "What a wonderful show. Your dance was lovely."

"Thanks!" I beamed.

"Did you see us out in the audience?" Megan asked.

"Yes!" I laughed. "Right when I popped out of the shell I spotted you."

"I could tell," Megan said. "You froze for a minute. You're not supposed to let the audience distract you."

Ugh. I could tell Megan didn't like the attention I was getting—especially from Vanessa.

"I'm sure she was supposed to do that," Lily said.

"Yes," I said, remembering something Vanessa had told me. "I was connecting with the audience. Engaging them in my story."

"That's exactly what you should do!" Vanessa said approvingly. "Megan, you can actually learn from that. In your dance, you need to be thinking about the audience and not just yourself."

Ha! Megan kind of deserved that, but I did feel a tiny bit of sympathy as her face fell.

"Hey, Harper!" I turned around to see Drew standing behind me. Then he turned to Vanessa. "Hi, are you Harper's mom?"

"Ah, no! Vanessa's my dance teacher," I said.

"Oh hey, Trina!" he noticed her. "Trina also helped us learn our dances."

Vanessa raised an eyebrow.

"Yeah," I said. "We helped out just a little bit."

"What? You both totally saved my life onstage," Drew said. He turned to Vanessa. "They seriously helped us."

"I'm glad to hear that," Vanessa said, although she still looked a little annoyed.

"Hello, I would have helped too if anyone had even told me about it," Megan jumped in. She gave him an appraising glance and then looked at me. "I wanted to tell you that you make a perfect prince. I'm Megan."

"Thanks," Drew said to her.

"She's on my dance team," I told him. "Lily and Riley also are on my squad."

"That's cool you all came to support Harper and Trina," Drew said. "A couple guys from my baseball team came, but only because our English teacher is giving them extra credit."

We all laughed.

"Well, see ya later," Drew said. "Nice meeting you."

"I didn't know you had a boyfriend," Megan said.

"What? I don't!" I protested.

"That's a discussion for another time. We won't keep you," Vanessa said. "Please let your choreographer know I was impressed with your dance."

"Tell Flounder I was impressed!" Trina said.

"I will!" I said. Vanessa and the Bunheads turned to walk away. I grabbed Lily.

"I can't believe you didn't tell me you were coming!" I said.

"I didn't even know!" Lily said. "I was going to come tomorrow, but just me. We all went to practice today and Vanessa was like, *Surprise! We're going to Harper's show—get in the car.* Megan and Riley were all grouchy about it, but I think they secretly enjoyed the show."

Cool! Megan turned around and shot Lily a side eye.

"We should go," Megan said. "We're already missing a lot of practice time for our solos."

"Megan," Vanessa said.

We all froze as we realized Vanessa had heard her.

"Not only are we here to support a team member's dance, but I hope you learned something from watching her today," Vanessa said. "Stage presence and audience engagement."

Really? REALLY?

"Let this motivate you," Vanessa said to Megan.

Vanessa turned back to go. Megan looked at me, scowling.

"Oh, I'm motivated," Megan whispered, this time making sure Vanessa couldn't hear her.

"Guess what?" I said back. "So am I!"

The Saturday night and Sunday's matinee shows also went really well, without any surprises. My parents and sister came again, and I think I did a good job. I wanted to just celebrate.

But it was bittersweet in its own way. Of course, the major pressure was that I knew that after the show, I, of course, had to go to DanceStarz to audition for my solo.

The other was that nobody else in the play had to do that, so they all made other plans.

"Can't you just come to the cast party?" Ariel asked me as she took off her stage makeup.

After the show was over, there was strike and a cast party.

Strike was when you helped break down the set and clean up the stage, and I felt bad about not helping everyone.

"I can't," I said. "My dance thing doesn't even start until seven, and it's a school night. I feel bad enough that I have to skip the strike. I'm so unhelpful."

"You helped us by teaching us to dance!" Courtney had overheard us.

"And just by filling in," Ariel agreed. "It would be fun to have you at the cast party, that's all. It's nice to hang out without the stress of the show hanging over us."

I sneaked a glance at Drew across the room. *Sigh.* There were many reasons I wished I could have gone to the party. It was over! *The Little Mermaid* was over.

Zora ran up to me.

"Aw, man, you're not going to the cast party at all?" Zora asked. I shook my head sadly.

"Can I have your attention?" Zora jumped up on one of the benches. "One of our cast has to leave early now! Let's give her some love! *The Little Mermaid* is over for Harper! Let's clap her out!"

Everyone started clapping to a beat. *Clap! Clap!*

"What's happening?" I asked Sebastian, who was next to me.

"Tradition!" he said. "The last time the actor leaves the set, you clap them out the door."

Oh! I smiled as everyone surrounded me and clapped. Some people yelled, "Thanks, Harper!" Others cheered and whistled. It felt really good. I felt a pang, like something special was ending.

"Good-bye, Harper!" Zora let out a small sob. "Good-bye forever!"

"Or until lunch tomorrow?"

Drew called that out and everyone stopped and laughed.

"See you at lunch!" I yelled back, and walked out the door to the sound of the applause—for me.

I relived the applause and warm feeling of the musical for one brief second before the door opened and my sister opened the cast door.

"Harper!" she yelled. "You have to go!"

"Okay, I just have to change out of my costume—"

"You're late!" she said.

Mrs. Elliott came in behind her.

"Harper," she said. "Your parents are waiting in the car out front. Hurry. You can bring your costume back tomorrow. Just go."

I raced into the DanceStarz lobby, already feeling discombobulated. I hadn't realized how late it was. A bunch of dancers who weren't on the Squad were milling about and heading into Studio A, the largest one with the little stage in it. That's where we'd be performing for everyone.

"Good luck, Harper!" one of the Minis called out.

I slowed down, trying to look like I had everything in control. I smiled and waved. Yup, under control, under control . . . As soon as I turned down the hallway to the smaller studios I pretty much lost control. I raced down to Studio D and practically skidded as I burst inside.

The Squad was getting ready. No—everyone was already

ready. Lily and the Bunheads were already in their costumes, with their hair and makeup on point. They were stretching on the floor.

"Oh, look who's here," Megan said. "The dancing mermaid. I see you're still in your outfit of glory."

"It IS an outfit of glory!" Trina said. "It's so pretty."

"Harper!" Lily ran right up to me. "I was starting to get worried! How was the show?"

"Great—I—"

"I have to tell you," Lily said. "Vanessa just made us draw numbers for our order tonight. You're first."

"First?" I said. "I go first? Ack. I have to get ready. Where are our costumes?"

"Studio C," Lily said. "The racks by the closet."

"Thanks," I said.

I raced to get my dress. I ran into the studio—and it was empty. Oh no, someone had moved the rack. I had to go find it.

I ran out into the hallway—and into Vanessa.

"Ah, you're here," she said.

"I'm sorry, I know I'm late, but—" I was about to ask where my costume would be, but she continued.

"I know you had your musical," Vanessa said. "Please note we all have conflicts and dance competition judges will not wait for anyone. You miss your dance, you don't compete. That said, we proceeded with the lineup and you'll be first, so you'll need to be ready to dance promptly at seven."

Which was in ten minutes. I didn't want her to think there was any way I wouldn't be ready, so I simply said: "I will be!"

As soon as she left, I ran back into Studio C and threw open the cabinets hoping to find my costume. Nothing. Maybe Lily had meant Studio B? I ran in there. Nothing. Oh no, oh no. I raced back into Studio D. Everyone looked up.

"Harper, you do know you're up first, right?" Megan asked.

"Okay, has anyone seen my costume?" I asked.

"Studio C!" Lily said urgently.

"It's not there," I said.

"Did you ask Vanessa?' Trina asked.

I shook my head. "I don't want to freak her out," I explain.

"Go ask Vanessa," Megan said. "Although, hmm, there's only a few minutes till showtime, so do you really want to alert her to your disorganization?"

"Megan. Riley. Do you know where my costume is?" I asked, phrasing my words very carefully.

"Nope, I do not," Megan said. Riley shook her head no too.

"Maybe someone moved it," Riley said. "Like maybe they

moved it because they thought it was so late that everyone had what they needed."

"You were late." Megan nodded. I noticed she was only wearing the top of her costume—the leotard top but without the long skirt.

"Wait, where's your skirt?" I asked, hoping it was somehow with my dress.

"She had a wardrobe malfunction," Riley pointed out.

"Okay, my mom is fixing it, all right?" Megan said defensively. "It's going to be fine. Look, I need to get my head in the game, here. Stop distracting me."

"But, guys, our team member has an emergency," Trina added earnestly. "We all need to help Harper."

"We're not team members right now, we're rivals. We only have five more minutes. I'm warming up," Megan said. Riley nodded.

"I'll help you look, Harper!" Lily jumped up.

"No, no!" I said. "You stretch. Trina, thanks, but seriously, you need to stretch."

It wouldn't be fair to get in the way of Lily's—or anyone's—opportunity to dance in the solo audition. But she ran over to me anyway.

"What are you going to do?" she asked.

"I guess skip it," I said miserably.

"Don't skip it!" Lily said. "Just put on a leotard!"

"I do keep one in my dance duffel," I sighed. "No, wait, it's in my car. Ugh, it's a plain pink leo that's probably all wrinkled. Well, it's better than nothing. I'll text my mom to bring it to me while I look."

This stunk. I didn't even know where to begin looking. I decided I'd better at least get my hair and makeup ready while I was waiting for either a miracle and someone to bring me my solo costume, or my mom to show up with my wrinkled mess. I went over to the other side of the room and sat down in front of the mirror. Fortunately, I still had my stage makeup on from the musical, and that would have to do. I swiped a quick splotch of pink gloss over my lips.

I dug through my duffel and found my hair elastics. I quickly swept my hair up into a high ponytail, and wrapped it halfheartedly in a topknot. My heart was pounding. This was a mess. I really wanted to make a good impression with my solo. The entire DanceStarz studio was going to see me in a wrinkled leotard, all frazzled up.

"Harper?" My sister stuck her head in the door. Then she

brightened. "Hi, Megan! Hi, Lily and Trina and Riley!"

"Don't distract them!" I ran up to her. "Sorry, sorry, I know you're being nice, but everyone is way stressed."

Then I saw what was in her hand.

"Hailey, that's my *Little Mermaid* costume," I said. "I need my leotard."

"Ew," she said. "That was all bunched up in the trunk. You don't want to wear that. Wear this! It's so pretty!"

I looked at the dress. I guess there was no reason I couldn't wear it. I mean, between this and the wrinkled leotard, I had a better shot of Vanessa letting me onstage in this, right?

"You're a genius," I told her. "You are a genius."

"I know," Hailey said. "You're welcome."

I raced back into the studio and pulled on the costume. I gave myself a quick look in the mirror. Okay. It would have to do. The dress definitely looked nice! I looked a little frazzled, but I didn't have any time to spare. I raced into the studio.

"Oh, that's so smart!" Lily said when she saw me. "Your costume from the musical!"

"So pretty!" Trina said. "You know, it looks a lot like Megan's!"

Megan's eyes narrowed as she looked at me.

"You can't wear that," she said. "That's not your solo costume."

"I don't have a choice," I said. "I can't find mine."

"Oh, but Megan, you love Harper's costume," Trina said. "It's why you made your mom sew pearls on your skirt so it would look like Harper's, right?"

"You did?" I asked.

"Whatever! But see you can't wear a dress that looks a lot like mine!" Megan said. "I'm going to get Vanessa!"

She jumped up and stormed out of the room. Everyone shot me panicky glances. I definitely didn't want her stirring up things with Vanessa. I ran out after Megan.

"Megan, don't!" I said. "We want Vanessa to think our team has our act together."

"No, we don't," Megan said. "You just want Vanessa to think you do. That's why you got her to go to your musical Friday night so you could be all *la la, look at me* onstage getting all the applause! Well, guess what? That's not fair! I focus on dance every day, I never miss rehearsals, and I definitely don't skip them for a class play!"

She whirled around and looked me straight in the eye.

"I deserve this solo! I've devoted everything to dancing here and you think you can come in and just take everything— even wearing practically the same dress as me."

"Megan," I said. "Remember, we talked about this before our last competition. I'm not trying to take everything from you. I just want a chance at the solo—"

"IT'S MY SOLO," Megan said. "The Bells left, I'm next in line, I'm the number one dancer here. You go dance at your school, 'kay? Oh good, there's Vanessa."

Vanessa was coming up the hall toward us. Oh, no.

"Vanessa!" Megan pointed at my dress.

"My costume is missing, so may I wear this?!" I said to Vanessa. "Please?"

"You're responsible for your costume being ready to go." Vanessa shook her head. "Well, the show must go on."

"But—" Megan protested.

"Megan, where's your skirt?" Vanessa interrupted her.

"Uh!" Megan stammered. "My mom is doing a last-minute fix! I don't go until last, so I have time!"

"What did I just say about costumes being ready? Both of you, very disappointing," Vanessa scolded. "Megan, I'm going to introduce all of you before your dance, so you have a little time. But not much."

Megan looked really upset. I couldn't really feel sorry for her since she'd thrown me under the bus.

"I'll go put it on," she squeaked.

"Harper, tell everyone to meet you in the hall now. I'll send someone to get you," she said. And she turned and walked away.

Whew. I'd gotten off easy. I took a deep breath. I went into the studio.

"Squad!" I announced. Lily, Trina, and Riley looked up. "It's time!"

Everyone had their game faces on as we stood in the hallway.

"Where's Megan?" Riley whispered.

"Getting her skirt," I told her. "Actually, there she is."

Megan came up the hallway, looking stressed. She held her skirt with one hand. Vanessa came up behind her.

"CALL TIME!

"The other students are seated on the floor of the studio," Vanessa said. "You'll all wait your turns—silently—in the small lounge attached to the studio. You'll each perform on the small stage. I will introduce you, and your song will begin. Harper, you're up first. Let me signal the sound person, and when I wave you in, enter."

We waited out in the hallway.

"This whole thing stinks," Megan said. "Why do we have to dance in front of everyone else to get our solo? Vanessa probably already knows who's she's going to pick. This is stupid."

One of the Minis arriving late hurried toward the studio. She stopped when she saw us.

"Hi, Squad!" she said, excitedly waving before she went inside. "Hi!"

I closed my eyes to get into the zone, but something was bothering me. "Wait. I know we're competing against one another, but we're still a team."

"So?" Riley said.

"So, I think we should keep up with our tradition," I said. "I know Megan said we're going in as rivals, but I think we're representing DanceStarz as the Squad."

"Yes," Trina said. "See how that Mini looked at us? Like we're role models."

"We need to act like it." Lily nodded.

"Let's huddle," I said quietly. Everyone, including a reluctant Megan, huddled. "Remember our corrections."

"Watch your feet," Trina whispered.

"Be high energy," Lily whispered.

Megan didn't say anything. But she didn't stop us either.

"Remember to connect with the audience," I whispered. "This is our first chance to tell our stories, individually, but together as the Squad."

"We're here to represent Vanessa and the DanceStarz Squad. Let's be thankful for this opportunity to dance!"

And Megan started our new ritual.

We whispered:

"Dance!" And did a little dance.

"Starz!" We fluttered our fingers like sparkling stars.

Then we leaned into a huddle and whispered:

"Squad!"

I smiled at my teammates. Then I stepped back. I wanted to have a few seconds for myself, to get in the zone. I closed my eyes and tried to picture myself dancing perfectly. Then I remembered the story.

Taking the leap!

I'd moved to Florida, into a new house, started at a new dance studio, auditioned onto the Squad, made new friends, joined the school musical, danced in the school musical, and was now auditioning for the very first solo. . . . I could show my journey with this dance. I knew I could be fearless here, too.

"From the Squad . . . Harper McCoy!" Vanessa announced from inside the room. The studio door opened, and I went in.

I took my place at the front of the room and struck my pose.

The room was packed with dancers, little kids up front and teenagers lining the walls. They were all staring at me.

Megan's mom was at the computer, doing the music. I saw Vanessa give her a signal to start, and I took a deep breath.

And I danced. I did my best to let me body feel the music and really let my mind feel the emotions. I let my energy pour out to the audience, especially to the little kids who someday might be part of the Squad. I wanted to connect with them, to tell them they could do it. Take the leap!

I spun, I twirled, I leapt!

And finished with my pose, strong and solid.

I did it!

I was breathing hard as I jumped up. Everyone was clapping like crazy for me, and I smiled gratefully. From the corner of my eye, I could see Vanessa also clapping but not letting her expression give anything away.

I walked with purpose out the door into the hallway.

I DID IT!

I was so happy it was over, when I saw the Squad I gave them each a big hug. Trina! Lily! Riley! Even Megan. I was so happy and relieved it was over, I would have hugged the Bells if they'd been there!

"Oomph," Megan said grumpily. And then I heard the sound of something small hit the floor.

"You lost a pearl," Trina pointed out.

"I know," Megan snapped. "Don't anyone touch me."

Clink! Another pearl fell off.

"Trina!" Vanessa came out and called up Trina next.

"Break a leg!" I whispered to her.

Clink! Clink! Clink!

Vanessa slowly turned around and frowned. She looked down at the floor.

"What was that?"

"Nothing," Megan said at the same time Trina said: "Some of the pearls from Megan's skirt."

"Are you having a problem with your skirt?" Vanessa asked.

"No!" Megan said. She stood completely still. I think she was even holding her breath.

"Lily, you're up," Vanessa said.

"Break a leg, Lily!" I told her.

Lily gave a little "Eek!" and followed Vanessa into the studio.

"This is just great! Now my skirt is falling apart and it's totally your fault, Harper!" Megan looked at me accusingly.

Wait, what?

"How can that possibly be my fault?" I asked.

"Well, I was in such a hurry to get ready because you were late tonight. It messed everything up, so I had to rush my mom sewing the pearls on my skirt," Megan said defensively.

How could she blame me for that?

"That's not my fault," I protested.

"Well, it kind of is," Riley shrugged. "Because the only reason Megan got the extra pearls to put on it is because she wanted her dress to be fancier after seeing your dress in the school musical. And good thing she did, since you snuck in your fancy costume to wear today."

"That's not what I did," I said. "I'm only wearing it because my solo costume went missing!"

"Actually, that's true." Riley frowned and looked at Megan. "If her costume hadn't gone missing, she wouldn't be in that dress that looks just like your dress."

"The point is, Harper ends up making us look bad," Riley continued.

"I don't think that's true." Trina frowned.

"It's true!" Riley said. "Harper makes me look bad by busting into DanceStarz and being a better dancer than us!"

"Well, wait, she's not a better dancer than us," Megan said. "At least me, Riley."

"Uh, that's not what I meant," Riley backtracked.

"Riley, you might be right," Trina said. "Megan, you flipped out last night after you saw Harper dance in *The Little*

Mermaid. Then you had to go copy her dress with the pearls on it. You're trying to be more like her. Harper, you should take it as a compliment."

"I'm not complimenting Harper! Harper gets enough compliments from Vanessa!" Megan said.

"Guys." I needed to stop this somehow. "Can we just chill?"

"Chill? How can I chill?" Megan was really worked up. "I'd better get this solo! Do you know how long I've wanted this? I was the very first dancer here at the studio, and I deserve it!" Megan was so upset she pounded the wall, and when she did it set off a chain reaction. Her skirt shook and pearls started flying everywhere. She grabbed at her skirt, which only made things worse.

Just then Vanessa came out the door, followed by Lily.

"Riley. You're up," Vanessa said.

And that's when it happened. Vanessa stepped on one of Megan's pearls. And she slid.

Oh no!

We gasped as Vanessa teetered and wobbled on her high heels, trying to regain her balance as she slid down the hallway, stepping on pearls and landing right on her butt.

We all stood there horrified. Thankfully, Vanessa was able to hop right back up and dust herself off, so she wasn't hurt.

Phew. But then she turned around slowly and looked at all of us.

"Sorry," Megan croaked.

Vanessa walked carefully toward us with a steely expression on her face.

"Riley," Vanessa said slowly. "As I was saying, you are up. However, Megan: obviously your dress provides a safety hazard not only to you"—she paused and glared—"but to others. Trina will be dancing next, and Megan, if you do not have an acceptable substitute for your costume in time, you will not be able to dance tonight. At all."

She opened the door to the studio and beckoned Riley in. Riley shot a panicky glance at Megan and then disappeared inside.

"Well, there goes my dream," Megan said. "I might as well give up dancing, period, the end."

"Can you just wear shorts with the top?" Trina asked.

"No, ugly." Megan started to sniff.

"Why don't you borrow one of our costumes?" Trina asked her.

"Oh sure, after you've already danced in them and everybody saw it," Megan said. "They'll laugh at me if I reuse your dress. My fans have high expectations for me."

I rolled my eyes at that comment and looked at Lily. She

shrugged. Part of me wanted to help Megan, but I also knew she'd dug herself into this hole. I'd been prepared to dance in a wrinkled leotard if I'd had to, just to make sure I at least got to dance. If Megan was going to be this picky, after being so mean to me . . . I was going to have no sympathy.

Then I saw tears forming in her eyes. Then she burst out crying.

"My mother is going to kill me. She thinks I'm the grand finale so Vanessa will announce I'm the soloist, and she's in there waiting for it!" Megan sobbed. "She was already mad at me that I went over budget on the dress! And then I made her sew on pearls! And she bought me a million private lessons with Vanessa, and if she did all that for nothing and I don't even get a solo she's going to be so mad at me. She'll know I screwed everything up!"

A few more pearls shook off and rolled down the hall. *Clink, clink, clink.*

"Aw, Megan." We all felt bad.

"Megan, I'm sorry that's going on," I said. I totally get being under pressure.

"Oh, give it up, Harper." Megan sniffled. "You should be happy that things fell apart for me, after I sabotaged you."

"You have been pretty rough with our duet," I said. Then I took a wild guess. "Too bad that nobody knows where my solo costume is, because I could let you borrow it to wear for your audition."

Megan froze.

Lily picked up on that very quickly. "Harper, that's such a nice gesture. It's too bad your dress is still missing."

"You'd really let me wear your dress?" Megan asked quietly.

"Yes, I actually would, because you are my teammate. We're the Squad and we should stick together," I said. "Even though you keep forgetting that."

"Look, it's not like I planned it," Megan said "The custodian asked me if I needed the costume, and I was honest. I didn't need it."

"But I asked you if you knew where it was," I said.

"But I don't!" Megan said. "I don't know where she took it."

"I can't believe you," Lily said. "You don't even deserve to dance today. You need to tell Vanessa so Harper doesn't get in trouble."

Megan cried harder. I'd never seen her like this. Ugh, ugh, ugh. I knew I'd feel guilty later if I didn't at least try to help her.

"Let's go see if we can find the custodian and my costume," I sighed. "Come on."

"Really?" Megan looked at me suspiciously.

"Yes, but only if you promise not to sabotage me anymore,"

I said. "If you're on my team, I have to be able to trust you. We have to trust each other."

Just then, Riley burst through the door.

"Nailed it!" she crowed. Then she saw Megan and dropped her grin. "Uh, I mean, sorry you can't dance."

"She's dancing," I said firmly. "Hurry, before Vanessa gets out here. We need to find the custodian and get my costume from the rack for Megan to wear."

"I told her," Megan said. "And from now on you have to be nice to Harper."

"Me?!" Riley looked taken aback.

"I'm going to convince Vanessa to wait a minute for you. Lily, Trina, can you help them?" They both nodded. "Hurry, go!"

They'd just rounded the corner of the hallway when Vanessa came out.

"Where is everyone?"

"They'll be right back," I said, my heart pounding.

"So Megan is not dancing?" Vanessa asked me.

For a split second, I thought of all the times Megan had been nasty to me and imagined myself saying *no*. I shook that thought out of my head. I could never do that.

"She is, she is!" I said. I needed to stall. "I know you said the show can't wait for anyone, but when I was dancing, I saw all those dancers in there looking at me and maybe some of them dream about being on the Squad someday so we all thought I could go in and say something, um, inspiring. That's why they left me here: so I could be, uh, the . . . spokesperson."

Oh, that sounded ridiculous. There was no way she was going to buy it. I could tell from her skeptical look that she wasn't buying it. But then she surprised me.

"I suppose that could be a nice addition to the evening," Vanessa said. "Go on and say something. You have a few minutes."

"Really?" I squeaked. "Great! Thanks!"

I scurried into the studio before she could change her mind. This was great! I was so happy she'd gone along with me! Until I stood up in front of the room and all the dancers were staring at me. And I didn't have anything prepared. Hmm. Maybe this wasn't such a good plan after all. After all of this, was I going to completely embarrass myself?

"Um. Hi," I said. And then Hailey popped up from the crowd and called out, "Hi, Harper!"

I could hear her whisper, "That's my sister."

And I had an idea.

"She's right. I'm Harper, Hailey's sister," I said. Hailey looked thrilled. "So I wanted to give you advice I gave her. Maybe some of you want to be on the Squad someday. You're all so talented!"

Some of the girls perked up, but I noticed others deflated.

"Okay, maybe you don't think you're talented in dance. Uh, maybe you're actually not talented."

People started to giggle.

"But even if you aren't, you shouldn't give up! You should work harder to get what you want. You can learn from your mistakes! Follow your dreams!" I said. Everyone looked at me, smiling. I think I'd pumped them up. *Woo hoo! Yeah!* I felt really good! But they were still looking at me! I didn't know what else to say! So . . . "So yeah! Okay!"

I stood up there, not sure what to do next. And the door opened. I was relieved that Megan was walking in. Except it wasn't Megan. . . .

Beep! Boop!

A small robot wheeled into the room. *Huh?* I looked at the door and saw Trina holding a remote control. I remembered she said at Robotics Club she'd been building a robot that could dance! Everyone turned and started smiling and pointing at it.

"Heh. Lo," the robot said robotically. "I am Star the dancing robot. Do you want to see me dance?"

"YES!" everyone yelled. And the robot started dancing! Well, not sure you'd call it dancing, but it moved left and right and spun around. *Boop! Beep! Boop!*

I ran out to the doorway, where Trina was hiding.

"Is that the robot you made?" I asked.

"Yes!" she said. "I had her in my mom's car, so I thought she could help distract until Megan got ready!"

"That's really cool you did that," I said. "You're really smart."

"Oh no, I'm not," Trina said. "It's just simple coding and the wiring. . . ."

Yeah, that was over my head. Just then Megan came running down the hall, followed by Lily and Riley. All three of them were out of breath. When Megan got close enough, I could see she was wearing my lavender costume.

"You found it!" I said. "It looks great on you."

At that moment, I knew what I had to say.

"I want to support you guys, my fellow DanceStarz dancers," I said, looking squarely at Megan. "We're all on the same team! We need to be here for each other!"

Beep! Boop! Star made its way offstage.

Megan confidently strutted out to the front of the room. She was in the dance zone as she struck her pose. Then Megan's mother yelled out her name super loudly. I saw Megan flinch. I ran off to the side of the room and tried to be quiet as the door closed and I was left to wait in the hallway with my other teammates.

We all sat on the floor, silently. Well, not all of us.

Beep! Boop!

The dancing robot explored Studio D, rolling around and occasionally twirling and emitting random noises.

"Can't you shut that thing up?" Megan grumbled to Trina.

"Don't hurt her feelings," Trina said. "She helped you tonight."

"You programmed her to help," Riley pointed out.

"Yeah," Lily said. "Trina helped out Megan and we helped out Megan but mostly Harper helped out Megan by letting her wear her costume."

We all were in our regular clothes, having quickly changed out of the costumes after Megan had finished her dance. We were waiting for Vanessa. And the big reveal.

Who would get the solo?

"You're going to get it," Riley told Megan. "You obviously killed it. I heard a crazy-loud cheer."

"That was my mother," Megan said miserably.

There was a pause of silence. Then I couldn't help it. I cracked up. That set everyone off.

"It's not that funny," Megan said.

"Yes, it is." I couldn't help laughing.

We all giggled. Even Megan cracked a tiny smile.

"Don't worry, I thought everyone was cheering my inspiring speech," I continued, "but it was really for Trina's robot who rolled in behind us."

Beep! Boop! the robot responded.

That just set everyone off again.

"How do you think I felt?" Megan said. "I was about to do my big dance and everyone was sad the robot had left."

"Maybe the robot should get the solo," I said.

"That robot cannot steal the solo," Megan said, sounding serious for a second. Then she jumped up, picked up the robot, and put it in a cabinet.

Beep! Boop! the robot chirped faintly.

We were dying laughing when Vanessa walked in the room.

Immediately we all got serious. It was time! Vanessa was going to announce the solo.

"I'm pleased to see you all laughing together," Vanessa said. "I also was pleased to see how you stepped up to help one another out tonight with your solos."

We smiled.

"However, I was not pleased with all of the shenanigans." Vanessa frowned.

We all stopped smiling.

"Dancing a solo is more than being the best dancer," Vanessa said. "I need someone I can rely on as well as who can deliver."

"I also can announce that our next competition will be regionals," Vanessa explained. "We will have one group dance with the Squad, two duets, and one solo."

We all fidgeted in our seats. This was a little too suspenseful for me!

"Our first duet will be: Trina and Riley."

Trina squealed happily and tried to high-five Riley, who wasn't as happy, having realized she was out of the running for the solo.

"Our second duet will be . . ." Vanessa paused.

This was it! This was it. I took a deep, calming breath.

"Harper—"

That was me. I didn't get the solo. Megan got the solo. Megan got it. After all that, Megan got it.

Okay, okay, regroup. Think of the bright side, I thought. Hopefully, that meant I'd have my first duet with Lily! Lily mouthed *Sorry* to me. She knew I was disappointed. We both went in for a hug.

"—and Megan," Vanessa said.

Lily and I both froze, arms out. *Wait, what?*

"WHAT?" Megan blurted out.

"Harper and Megan, you'll be our second duet," Vanessa said calmly. "And our first DanceStarz soloist is . . . LILY!"

Lily?

I could see the entire Squad in the mirror, and we all had the same look on our faces. Shock. Especially Lily.

"Lily!" I yelled, the happiness bubbling over my disappointment. "You got the solo!"

I leaned over and gave her a huge hug. Trina did the same.

"Vanessa!" Megan looked like she hadn't processed it yet. "I'm . . . Wait, what?"

"I don't need to explain myself," Vanessa said sternly. "However, I would like to share some reasons why Lily will be representing DanceStarz in our first solo. Lily has been consistent. She has taken on extra practices and worked extremely hard to improve her skills. This shows me responsibility and reliability. She also took on a challenge outside her comfort zone by doing tumbling instead of ballet."

"BUT—" Megan started to protest.

"And she doesn't complain about things," Vanessa added pointedly.

Megan snapped her mouth shut.

Wow. Lily!

"Go, Lily!" I cheered and began clapping for her. I was so happy! Everyone, even Megan, began clapping too.

Beep! Boop! Robot chirped again from the closet.

"Even the robot is cheering for you!" Trina said happily.

Vanessa looked around, confused, and then sighed and shook her head.

"Um," Lily said shyly. "Thank you, Vanessa. Thanks, Squad. I definitely wasn't expecting this, but I promise to represent DanceStarz and the Squad best I can."

Lily's face was shining. I thought about all the times she'd been rehearsing and overlooked so far. Now she finally had her big moment! I reached out and grabbed her hand and squeezed it.

"Excellent," Vanessa said.

"My mother is going to kill me," Megan muttered under her breath.

"Your mother . . ." Vanessa had heard the comment. Megan flinched. ". . . is going to be quite busy, as I've asked her to assist me."

I couldn't tell from the look on Megan's face if that was a good or bad thing. Probably bad.

"Which brings me to my next announcement," Vanessa continued.

Another big announcement?

"After regionals, we will head to another competition," Vanessa said. "Our first nationals. And nationals will be in New York City!"

NEW YORK?! Now we all cheered! Nationals! And we got to travel! Traveling competitions were so much fun—staying overnight in a hotel together and seeing the city between the competition events. And New York! It was like going home for me!

"That's why Megan's mother—and a few others who I'm waiting to hear from—will be coming on the trip to help. And by the way, I'll be picking a soloist for that one too," Vanessa said.

"Yessss!" Megan pumped her hand. More solos! Solos in the big league this time.

"So let's learn from today and get ready to work harder than you've worked so far," Vanessa said.

I knew I'd be ready. *NYC, here I come!*

"Now go get some rest," Vanessa said. "See you all tomorrow at Squad rehearsal."

The door shut.

"Wow," Riley said. "That was a lot."

Yeah. That was a lot.

"I, uh, yeah," Lily said, still in shock. "I think I need some time to process this. Sorry?"

"Don't apologize," I said. "You earned it, and you deserve it."

"Plus, I'm going to get the solo for nationals," Megan said. "So, haters, back off."

We all looked at her.

"I'm kidding!'" she said. "Kind of."

"Nationals!" I said. "You guys, we get to travel together! We get to go to New York City together! This is going to be amazing."

We all jumped around, excited. The Squad was going to NYC!

"All right, I'm tired of you people." Megan yawned. "I'm out."

We all went to get our stuff from the cubbies. I noticed

my lavender dress was placed very neatly on my duffel.

Megan said what I was thinking: "I have so many alerts my phone is beeping more than Trina's robot." Then she paused. "OH, GREAT. OH, JUST GREAT."

"What?"

"Guess who also is going to nationals?" Megan said. "The BELLS."

"Oh, noooo," we all groaned.

"We have to beat the Bells!" Megan said fiercely. "We're not going to sleep! We are going to practice every single day, every spare minute! Maybe we should start now—"

"Can we elect somebody else team captain?" I yelled out.

"How about Trina's robot?" Lily said. "All in favor, raise your hand."

Everyone except for Megan's hand shot up.

"Seriously?" Megan said. "Fine. You get the night off. But tomorrow—"

"Tomorrow I have plans!" I said. I needed a break! But also, I wanted to spend some time with Lily. FUN time. Maybe swimming, or if she had to work, I'd help her out at Sugar Plums. But I got what Megan was saying. "Tuesday, though, for sure."

"Fine." Megan sighed dramatically.

I turned on my phone and saw I had a bunch of messages, too. And then my phone went *blllllrp* with a video call. I smiled and answered.

"PEARL!" It was Zora! "We wanted you to be part of the cast party! Everyone say hi to Harper!"

Awwwww!

She held the camera over her head so I could see a flash of faces go by. Ariel and Flounder and Courtney and the fish and the humans! Drew flashed me a peace sign!

"HI!" I waved back happily. "Hi!"

"We miss you!" they all yelled. *Aw!* I was so happy they missed me!

"I'm at the dance studio! Say hi to my musical cast!" I held up the phone toward the Squad.

"Hiii!" They all waved.

"Hi, everyone! Hey, I see you, Flounder!" Trina called out.

"Hi, Prince Eric!" Megan called out.

Hmm. I turned the phone back around quickly.

"Okay, I'll see you all at school!" I said.

"You did awesome at your solo!" Zora said, just before the video disconnected.

"For the musical, maybe. But not for the dance audition!" Megan said enough. We all gasped. "Oh, chill out. I was just kidding. I didn't get it either. Lighten up."

"Well, we all can be proud of our teammate Lily," I said. "Can we go over quick to Sugar Plums for celebration fro-yo?"

"Ooh, Megan, can we?" Riley needed permission.

"A smoothie does sound kind of good," Megan admitted. "I'm going to get a scoop of protein in it. I need all the strength I can get to prepare for my solo at nationals."

"Your solo at nationals?" I raised my eyebrow at her.

"Yup," Megan said casually. "I may even wear your purple costume for it. It did look good on me. . . ."

Thwap! I tossed my dance towel at her. There was a pause and then *thwap! Thwap!* The rest of the Squad—even Riley— tossed theirs at her too.

Everyone, especially Megan, was laughing.

"This is all sinking in. Can you believe we're going to New York City?!" Trina said, grabbing Star from the closet.

"For Harper, it's like going home again," Lily said. "Well, close to home."

"I know, I'm so excited! Maybe I can see some of my old

dance . . . team. . . ." My voice trailed off as I realized something. I went to my old dance team's website and clicked on a link I used to check all the time.

It read:

UPCOMING EVENTS!

Blah, blah, blah . . . and there it was. *NATIONALS, NYC.*

I'd be competing against my old team. Whoa. What if I got the solo? Can you imagine?

The announcer would say: "Please welcome to the stage, from DanceStarz, Harper!"

I would walk onto the stage, in MY lavender costume, head held high. I'd get into my opening pose as the music began . . . five . . . six . . . seven . . . eight!

And I would dance! And I would *win*! And—

I opened my eyes and looked at my Squad. Yes. I could imagine it.

*T*his book is about TEAMWORK, so first I want to thank the team who helped bring this book to life:

• The WME|IMG team: Sharon Jackson, Mel Berger, Jenni Levine, Erin O'Brien, Joe Izzi, Matilda Forbes Watson, Josh Otten, Lisa DiRuocco, and everyone at WME|IMG for your support and encouragement.

• The Aladdin team: Starting with Alyson Heller, the driving force behind this book—thank you so much! And to Mara Anastas, Laura DiSiena, Jodie Hockensmith, Nicole Russo, and everyone at Simon and Schuster Children's/Aladdin for your hard work and dedication.

• Rachel Rothman, who has believed in me from the very beginning and was invaluable making this book so awesome!

• Katie Greenthal, Marisa Martins, and everyone at the Lede Company for being such awesome publicists and helping bring my voice out to the world.

• Scott Whitehead and everyone at McKuin, Frankel, Whitehead for all of your wise legal advice.

And:

• Julia DeVillers!! You gave Harper (and the rest of the DanceStarz) an amazing voice and it has been so fun to see these characters come to life. A million thank yous for being such a smart, savvy, and fun partner on this project!

This book is about DANCE, so of course I want to thank all of my friends who have supported me every dance step of the way:

• Sia, who shows me how to be the person I want to be

• All of my dance teachers, who have taught me to be the best I can be

• All of the dancers who have ever shared the dance floor and stage with me. You've motivated and inspired me!

This book is about FAMILY, and you know I love my family so much!

• Kenzie!! My creative and talented sister. You're my best friend and I love you!!

• Gregga, who has always been there for me, supported me and made sure I have whatever I need with patience and positivity—and no complaints!

• Jane, Lilia, and Jack Buckingham, who make LA feel like my home.

• Michelle Young, for all the sleepovers, loud music in the car, and the laughter that never ends.

And:

Mom!! don't know how I got so lucky to have you as my mom. Thank you for everything.

This book is about FOLLOWING YOUR DREAMS. To anyone who has ever watched me, come out to meet me, bought my books and cheered me on as I pursue my passions and follow my dreams in dance, acting, fashion design, makeup, the arts—and just living my life . . .

I want you to know I'm cheering you on, too. I love what I do so much, so thank you for sharing the journey with me. I love you!

Maddie

Don't miss the next book:

THE COMPETITION

"Welcome to . . . regionals!" the announcer's voice rings throughout the packed convention center.

This is it. Regionals. And all eyes are on us. This is the moment! We are here! My costume is super cute. It's black and pink, with some flowy ribbons dangling off my shoulders. That sounds weird, but it works. I have a little hat on my head, tilted just right and securely fastened by approximately a thousand bobby pins.

At least I hope it's securely fastened. That would be bad if my hat fell off, wouldn't it? Ha! Okay, that's actually not funny. If my hat falls off, then I might trip over it. Or one of my dance squad might trip over it, and slide all the way across the stage—not just across the stage! Off the stage! Onto the judge's table, knocking everything over and destroying the entire regionals!

My best friend and teammate, Lily, grabbed my hand and squeezed it hard, snapping me out of my imaginary list of things that could go wrong.

"Harper!" Lily whispered to me. "I think my hat is loose!"

"I was JUST thinking mine was," I whispered back.

"That's why we're best friends," Lily said. "You understand me."

Lily and I had become best friends ever since I'd moved to Florida. Lily, who had been new to the team too, was the first person I met, right before we'd auditioned for DanceStarz. I remember when I walked in, I was worried I'd never find my place on the team. The rest of the team, aka the Bunheads—Megan, Riley, and Trina—hadn't exactly been welcoming at first, to either of us. So Lily and I had bonded over that, and then become true friends, totally on the same page. Like for example, worrying about our hats falling off.

"Were you also thinking you'd trip on it, slide across the stage, and fall on the judges and the competition would come to a screeching halt and the judges would toss you out the door of the building?" I whispered.

"Um, no?" Lily said. "I take it back. I guess I don't under-stand you."

We both cracked up a little.

"Are you two laughing? No laughing!" Megan hissed at us. "This is serious business. Regionals."

When I'd first met Megan, I'd been intimidated by her. We'd had our ups and downs, but now we had mutual respect for each other's talent and hard work. We even had fun together. Most of the time.

"First this, and then our duet," Megan said, looking hard at me. "Serious business."

Okay, this was not one of those fun moments. Megan also was very competitive and intense—and my duet partner. Lily and I smiled at each other. It had taken a little while, but we had learned not to let Megan get to us before a competition.

"You're on deck, DanceStarz!" A woman with a clipboard came backstage.

Eek! This was it!

We all gathered around in a tight circle to do the ritual we'd made up as a squad.

"Dance!" Trina led the cheer.

Lily, Megan, Trina, Riley, and I all did a little dance move.

"Starz!" Trina continued.

We fluttered out fingers like sparkling stars. Then we leaned into a huddle and said:

"Squad!"

DanceStarz Squad was ready to take the stage! *HERE WE GO!*

"Make some noise for . . . DanceStarz!" the announcer's voice boomed throughout the packed convention center.

On that cue, we flashed out best smiles and stepped onstage in formation, our arms swinging in perfect sync. We sashayed to our positions, and we struck a pose and waited under the hot lights for the music. I had one hand on my hip and one in the air, steady. I took a moment to take it all in—the excited charge in the air, the supportive cheers. Yes. This was it. We'd worked so hard to get to this point. We'd edged out the fiercest including the team from competitive Energii, our biggest rivals. All that would be left for us to do is perform our hearts out. A solid show here would advance us to nationals, which—

Which I couldn't think about right now. I had to focus and go into my zone. This is when all of my training, my muscle memory, all of those hard rehearsals pay off. My brain shuts down, and my body takes over.

The music began. And I danced. We used to watch ourselves in the dance studio mirrors, but now the crowd is our only reflection. From the roar of the crowd, we were delivering the goods. Our leg extensions must have been showing off the flowy chiffon trailing from the backs of our shoulders. The pretty fabric swirls looked like a ribbon dance. Finally, that last beat dropped. We bowed and trotted offstage to extended applause.

Vanessa was the first to greet us offstage. "Beautiful," she said, beaming proudly. She's our dance team teacher and our choreographer AND owner of the DanceStarz Studio. We all grabbed one another in a big hug and jumped around to celebrate.

We got two seconds of celebrate before Vanessa cleared her throat.

"Duets, get ready."

Annnnd our killer performance was already a thing of the past. Lily and I went to give each other extra hugs.

"You got this," she whispered.

"Same!" I told her. It's a huge day for Lily. She got picked to be the solo dancer, and will be going last.

"Harper!" Megan hissed at me. "Let's go!"

I rushed to the shared backstage changing area to change costumes, into the sparkly deep purple leotard we picked out together. The farther we walked away from the rest of the squad, the more tense it felt to be alone with Megan.

"Remember," she said. "Vanessa changed the high kick in the end to a split jump."

"Yeah," I agreed. "And don't forget the arabesque to the new twirl move."

"I know that. Don't worry about whether *I* have all our moves down," she said dismissively. "Concentrate on yourself."

"You started this," I said, annoyed. "Duets are all about

making sure we're both on the same page. We have to help each other shine."

Megan snorted. I knew what was bothering her—again. She was still bitter that she didn't get the first-ever solo. We all had wanted that solo—but I was still super happy for Lily.

"It's Lily, not us, in the solo today," I reminded her.

"That doesn't mean I can't prove that I'm solo material," Megan muttered.

So that was her plan. She wanted to stand out in the duet in the hopes she'd get the next solo. That's a risky move, because nowhere in the word "duet" are the letters *s-o-l-o*. And, PS, the next solo was a big one, because it was nationals! Yes, if we placed high enough today, then we got to go to nationals and nationals this year . . . in NEW YORK CITY!

Then again, Megan has a point. The only person I should focus on was myself at the moment. I wanted to finish strong at regionals. I didn't want to let down the Squad! I didn't want let down DanceStarz, the studio I represent! And I didn't want to let myself down! I worked too hard for this.

We headed down the hall to the changing rooms. Regionals dressing rooms were an upgrade from the local competition. DanceStarz had our own corner, and Megan's and my mom were waiting for us.

"Great job, sweetheart!" My mom gave me a big hug. "Did you have fun?"

"Fun?" Megan's mother turned around. "This is not time for chitchat. They need to get ready for their big duet."

Mom raised an eyebrow at me.

"Don't engage," I whispered.

"Don't let her add to your stress." Mom smiled at me. Then she frowned. "Where are the girls' costumes?"

"Oh, I had my assistant do a last-minute steaming," Megan's mother said. "No wrinkles, only perfection. She's bringing them in now."

We went and sat down in front of the tables set up with mirrors. Megan and I didn't say anything while our moms helped us with our hair—except for the occasional "ouch" when the bobby pins got yanked out of our hat heads. My mom cleaned up all the pins and took the hat. We both know, though, that I'm better at doing my own hair than she is, so she let me finish. My hair was a little ratty from the bobby pins, so I brushed it out and pulled it up into a high ponytail.

"Mom?" I called her over and swung my pony back and forth.

"Wispie-free!" she said. "Nice and smooth."

"Where are our leotards? She is taking forever." Megan was

complaining. Megan's mom's assistant (I still couldn't believe she had an assistant) walked in with our leotards on hangers. "Give me mine!"

Megan grabbed hers, and then the assistant handed me mine. It was really pretty—a burgundy long-sleeved leotard we wore with a matching vest that had crystals embellished on it. It also was warm from being steamed.

"Break your legs!" my mom called out and left with Megan's mom to head to their seats in the audience.

I pulled on my costume—and noticed something weird. The leotard sleeves seemed a little long. *Huh.* Maybe steaming wrinkles out lengthened them. Megan came over wearing an identical outfit and ponytail.

"You look great," I told her. She was pulling at her sleeve. "Hey, is your sleeve bugging you, too? Mine feels stretched out."

"No," Megan said, pulling at her other sleeve.

"Why are you pulling at it?" I asked her.

"I think my arms grew. Yes! My arms may have lengthened because I've been doing all of my stretches in preparation for today. It will make my lines look amazing."

"Wait, if your sleeves are weird too, then—"

"Really? You're complaining right before our duet? Are you

trying to bring me down with your negative energy?" Megan asked me.

"What? No, I just thought it's weird that—"

Vanessa walked in the door. She looked at us both and immediately picked up the tension.

"Let's see that partnership shine out there," she said. "Any missteps will be more obvious, so remember you're in this together, girls."

"Yes, Vanessa." We both nodded, our ponytails bobbing.

Megan pretty much should have said *No, Vanessa*. When we took the stage, the music started—and Megan went into solo mode.

Step, high kick, and . . . What in the world was going on?! Megan took an extra step forward, hogging the spotlight. I tried to give her a side eye, but she gave me a toothy smile back. Her face was wide-eyed and expressive, working the audience. There was hardly any connection between us. The only connection I was feeling was between her and the audience. I guessed I had to just focus on myself. I twirled (yes, twice), did my turn series, and kicked. Then we got ready for our signature partner trick. This one relied on us being perfectly in sync.

Megan did a leap toward me, looking like she was going to

crash into me. I knew the audience would be at full attention, and so did Megan. She gave them a dramatic, overly surprised face. Then she slid forward on the ground so that she was right underneath my leg. Just as my leg would have hit her, she melted down into a hinge.

I twirled my leg horizontally over her, and then popped up. Then I twirled back over her, and she ducked down over and over. I finished with a turn holding my leg high and straight, with Megan underneath me, and held it for a few seconds. We did it perfectly! Yes! Whew! Then I brought my leg down and spun. Megan stepped in front of me, which by then I was getting used to. But that's when it happened.

Megan did a big swoop with her arm. She overdid her arm reach and tore her long-sleeved leotard, just under her arm. The seam split. She froze.

I couldn't help it: My first thought was *Serves you right.* My second thought was what Vanessa said, though—we are partners, and we're supposed to support each other. My third thought was that if Megan looks bad, I look bad.

My fourth thought was: *How do we cover it up?* I think that was Megan's only thought, from her panicky look.

When we spun with our backs to the audience, I mouthed to her: *I got you.*

I adjusted our dance and took action, positioning myself to cover her holey-ness with my body. Megan regrouped to let me block her. The result was a synchronized mirror image of poses that unfolded pretty well.

We ran offstage. Megan was clutching her arm. Riley and Trina were waiting in the hall, hair in buns, dressed in pink-and-butter-yellow dresses for their duet.

"Megan, you were awesome," Riley said.

"I can't believe this happened!" Megan was visibly upset. She ripped off the vest and threw it on the floor. "I'm suing the costume place."

"Oh, no!" Trina said. "Because they got your name wrong?"

"Huh?" We all looked at her, confused.

Trina picked up the vest off the floor and showed it to us. The label pinned into it said HARPER.

"Wait," I said. I pulled my vest off. Sure enough, it said MEGAN. No wonder my sleeves didn't fit—Megan had longer arms than I did.

"Harper wore my outfit, and my sleeve ripped!" Megan wailed. "It screwed up everything."

"WHAT?" I protested. "You're the one who grabbed it after your mother's assistant—"

"Oh. Whatever. That doesn't matter," Megan said. "What matters is my leo ripped onstage at regionals."

I saw Vanessa waving pointedly at us.

"Actually, I think what matters is Riley and Trina's duet onstage," I said, tilting my head toward Vanessa.

"Where are your priorities? I am not very happy right now," Megan snarled.

"I won't be happy either if our next duet doesn't take the stage on time," Vanessa said from behind us. Megan's face turned white.

"I meant, Riley! Trina! Go, team, go!" Megan recovered quickly.

Megan and I were done, so we went into the audience. All the parents were in seats. My little sister, Hailey, was waving at me to sit next to her. I went up the aisle and started to slide into the seat.

"Not you, Harper," she said. "I was saving the seat for Megan!"

Blugh. Megan turned around and smirked at me. Hailey loved Megan. Megan was actually really good with younger kids. On the bright side, I didn't have to sit next to my sister, who wiggled a lot.

I slid into a seat behind my mom. We all watched Riley and Trina do their jazz solo, cheering them on. They did great!

Trina was on point as always with her precision and her footwork, and Riley really worked the crowd.

"Go Riley! Go Trina!" I called out.

When the next duet came out, I heard Megan give an audible sigh.

"Let's give it up for a duet from the studio Energii!" the announcer called out. The two girls who came out were the Bells. They used to be on the DanceStarz competition team until they went to a new studio. They also had been Megan's teammates and so-called best friends. They hadn't been particularly nice to any of us since I'd moved here. They took the stage and did a modern routine that was truly impressive. When the crowd went wild for them, I clapped loudly, but Megan was subdued watching them dance. I knew it must hurt when your friends moved on.

It made me think about my friends from my old dance team in Connecticut. We still talked and liked each other's stuff on social, but I wondered what it would be like if I saw them in person. Would they have moved on? Would it hurt? Would I find out soon?